A
FAVOURITE
TREASURY
—— *of* ——
CHILDREN'S
STORIES

VIKING

Published by the Penguin Group
Penguin Books Ltd, 27 Wrights Lane, London W8 5TZ, England
Penguin Putnam Inc., 375 Hudson Street, New York, New York 10014, USA
Penguin Books Australia Ltd, Ringwood, Victoria, Australia
Penguin Books Canada Ltd, 10 Alcorn Avenue, Toronto, Ontario, Canada M4V 3B2
Penguin Books (NZ) Ltd, Private Bag 102902, NSMC, Auckland, New Zealand

Penguin Books Ltd, Registered Offices: Harmondsworth, Middlesex, England

On the World Wide Web at: www.penguin.com

First published as *The Puffin Treasury of Children's Stories* by Viking 1996
Published as *A Favourite Treasury of Children's Stories* by Viking 1998
This abridged edition published 2000
1 3 5 7 9 10 8 6 4 2

Printed in Singapore by Tien Wah Press (PTE) Ltd

British Library Cataloguing in Publication Data
A CIP catalogue record for this book is available from the British Library

ISBN 0–670–89354–4

A
FAVOURITE
TREASURY

— *of* —

CHILDREN'S
STORIES

CONTENTS

∾

Hans Christian Andersen

THE EMPEROR'S NEW CLOTHES

RETOLD BY WENDY COOLING

ILLUSTRATED BY IAN BECK

ONCE upon a time in a distant land there lived an Emperor who was known the world over for his extraordinary love of fine clothes. All his riches were used to buy the most beautiful silks, satins, brocades, laces and trimmings, and to pay the cleverest and most creative tailors in the land. He was the leader of fashion.

Unlike other kings and emperors he was not interested in his army, although he did like his soldiers to look splendid when they escorted him on royal visits. He was bored by government and left his ministers to run the country. All the Emperor cared about was showing off his latest outfits and appearing in public looking finer and richer than anyone else. He was always changing his clothes, sometimes a dozen times a day and, although most rulers are to be found in their council chambers, this Emperor was always sure to be in his wardrobe!

In the Emperor's city, life was full of pleasure and many visitors came to enjoy the parties and the theatres — and sometimes to swindle the honest citizens.

One day two clever swindlers arrived in town. They claimed to be weavers and said they could weave the finest cloth imaginable. They claimed that their colours were as delicate as butterflies' wings, their cloth as light as gossamer and their patterns

beautiful and unusually intricate. But more than this, they declared that their cloth had a magical quality and was invisible to all who were particularly stupid, or not fit to do the jobs they had been given.

The wild claims of the swindlers soon reached the ears of the Emperor and he was intrigued. 'The cloth would make the most wonderful clothes,' he thought, 'and how splendid it would be to tell the wise from the stupid amongst my people.' The more the Emperor thought about the cloth the more irresistible the claims of the swindlers became and he summoned them to his palace.

'Weave the cloth at once,' commanded the Emperor, already longing to show off to his people a fabric the like of which had never been seen before.

The swindlers asked for their money in advance, then they set up two looms and pretended to begin their work. They ordered golden threads and fine silks which went straight into their bags, and they pretended to weave at their empty looms. They worked day and night, talking to no one.

Soon the Emperor was anxious to know how the weaving was going. Although he was quite confident of his own cleverness and was sure he would be able to see the magic cloth, he felt a little too uneasy to go to the looms himself. Instead he sent his wise old Minister, a man he trusted completely and was very fond of, thinking, 'He's a clever man who does a good job, he will surely see the fabric and report back to me.'

The Minister went rather nervously to inspect the weaving, concerned because by now the whole city had heard of the magic quality of the cloth and everybody was talking about it.

The swindlers invited the Minister into their room saying, 'Don't you love the pattern and the shine of the cloth? Have you ever seen such colours?' But the Minister could see nothing.

The wise old man peered closely at the looms and put out a hand to feel the cloth, but there was nothing there. 'Can it be that I am stupid?' wondered the Minister. 'I have never thought so before, but if I am I must be careful to let no one know – for surely I am not unfit for my job.'

'What is your opinion of the cloth, Minister?' asked one of the swindlers. 'Is it not the most splendid design you have ever seen?'

'Oh yes,' replied the Minister. 'It is truly amazing. The colours are dazzling and the cloth is finer than I would have thought possible. I shall go and tell the Emperor at once how much I admire it.'

The swindlers described the cloth in great detail and the

Minister listened carefully so that he could repeat their words to the Emperor – and that is just what he did.

The swindlers demanded more money, more golden thread and silk, and pretended to work still longer at their looms. But the thread and silk went straight into their pockets and the looms were empty.

Soon the Emperor, impatient to know how the work was going, sent another honest man to check on progress.

'Isn't it looking wonderful?' remarked one of the swindlers as the official came in to inspect the cloth. But the official too could see nothing and, like the Minister before him, dared not admit it. How could he say he had seen only empty looms and still be considered wise?

'I am sure I am good at my job,' he thought. 'I am not stupid, but I can't risk honesty.' And so, like the Minister, he spoke in glowing terms of the wonderful cloth he could not see and the extraordinary designs that did not exist.

Now everyone was talking about the cloth and the whole city was buzzing with excitement. The Emperor could wait no longer and went with some of his courtiers and the Minister and the official who had been before to see the magical cloth for himself.

The swindlers as usual were only pretending to weave, and still their looms were empty. The two men who had visited before quickly pointed out the wonders of the material that they thought perhaps the others could see.

The Emperor looked at the empty looms and was shocked, but he managed to keep his face expressionless. 'I can see nothing!' he thought. 'Can it be that I am stupid? Am I not fit to be Emperor?'

He looked closer and closer and could still see nothing. Soon,

University of Chichester

Borrowed items 18/06/2019 19:15
XXXX5831

Item Title	Due Date
* favourite treasury of children's stories	12/07/2019

* Indicates items borrowed today

www.intellident.co.uk
email support@intellident.co.uk

like the others before him, he was nodding his head in approval and saying, 'Yes, it is very beautiful. It is unlike anything I have seen before.' How could he admit he could see nothing and be thought a fool?

The courtiers with him, desperate to be thought wise, all praised the cloth although they too could see nothing. They spoke in turn, each more extravagantly than the one before. Cries of 'Amazing!' 'Wonderful!' 'Spectacular!' 'Unbelievable!' 'Superb!' echoed around the chamber.

The Emperor ordered the swindlers to make him some clothes out of the cloth to wear at a great procession due to take place the next week. To show his delight and approval he gave each swindler a medal, the Emperor's Cross, to wear from his buttonhole, and he declared them to be Lords of the Loom.

The swindlers pretended to work all through the night right up

to the day of the procession, burning sixteen candles at the window so that the people of the city could see them. They pretended to take the cloth from the loom, to cut out the invisible garments with a huge pair of scissors and to work away with needles and thread. At last, as the morning of the procession came, they announced, 'The clothes are ready. Let the Emperor know.'

The atmosphere was tense as the Emperor entered the room. The swindlers held the invisible garments against him, asking him to admire the coat, the trousers and the cloak with its long flowing train. They remarked on the lightness of the garments. 'They are so light,' they said, 'it will feel as though you have nothing on at all.'

The confident swindlers smiled at everybody in a relaxed fashion. 'May we now dress Your Majesty in the new clothes?' asked one, and the Emperor slowly took off his clothes.

The swindlers helped him into his new, invisible trousers, jacket and cloak and the Emperor looked into the mirror, still able to see nothing. His servants admired his clothes saying, 'You look wonderful, Your Majesty, the fit is perfect.' But still the Emperor could see nothing.

The Emperor took his place under a plumed canopy and waited for the grand procession to begin. 'Doesn't the suit shimmer in the sunlight,' he commented to his courtiers. In return they mentioned the exquisite fit of the clothes and the lightness of the material.

In the city the people thronged the streets, all of them remarking on the beauty and quality of the Emperor's new clothes. No one wanted to be thought stupid. No one admitted that they could not see the clothes.

The Emperor's procession made its way through the town and seemed to be a huge success until, suddenly, a little child who knew nothing of adult pride, called out, 'The Emperor has nothing on!'

The boy's father said, 'Listen to the voice of an innocent child.'

Whispers spread through the crowd. Voices could be heard saying, 'He has nothing on!' or 'Listen to the child!' Soon the voices were louder and were crying, 'The Emperor has nothing on!' and the Emperor knew that it was true. He knew he had been fooled. But he was a proud man and although inside he cringed with embarrassment, he held himself straight and walked on with dignity, and his gentlemen-in-waiting walked proudly behind him, holding the lighter than cobweb train that really was not there at all.

∾

Margaret Mahy

THE RUNAWAY REPTILES

ILLUSTRATED BY TONY ROSS

S IR Hamish Hawthorn, the famous old explorer, was not
happy.

'Oh, Marilyn,' he cried to his favourite niece. 'I long to go
exploring up the Orinoco river once more, but who will look after
my pets?'

'The Reverend Crabtree next door will feed the cats, I'm sure,'
said Marilyn. 'He is a very kind-hearted man. And I will take care of
the alligator for you.'

'But Marilyn,' Sir Hamish said, 'what about your neighbour? He
might object to alligators.'

Marilyn lived in Marigold Avenue – a most respectable street.
The house next door was exactly the same as hers. It had the same
green front door, the same garden and the same marigolds. A man
called Archie Lightfoot lived there. He was rather handsome, but
being handsome was not everything. Would he enjoy having a
twenty-foot Orinoco alligator next door?

'Don't worry, Uncle dear,' said Marilyn. 'I shall work something
out.'

At that exact moment, by a curious coincidence, Archie Lightfoot was opening an important-looking letter.

Dear Mr Lightfoot, he read.
Your great-aunt – who died last week – has left you her stamp album, full of rare and valuable stamps.

'Terrific!' shouted Archie. Though he had never met his great-aunt, he had inherited her great love of stamps. Now, it seemed, he had inherited her stamp album as well. He read on eagerly.

There is one condition. You must give a good home to your aunt's twenty-foot Nile crocodile. If you refuse, you don't get the stamp collection. Those are the terms of the will.

'What will Marilyn Hawthorn say?' muttered Archie Lightfoot. 'A beautiful girl like that will not want a twenty-foot Nile crocodile on the lawn next door. I will have to work something out.'

That night, Marilyn Hawthorn tossed and turned. She could not sleep. In the end she decided to get up and make herself some toast. She could see the light next door shining on the marigolds. Archie Lightfoot was evidently having something to eat as well.

There is something about midnight meals that makes people have clever ideas. Sure enough, on the stroke of twelve, Marilyn Hawthorn suddenly thought of the answer to her problem.

The next day she ran up a large blue sun bonnet and a pretty shawl on her sewing machine, and borrowed the biggest motorized wheelchair she could find. Then she went round to her uncle's house.

Before leaving for the Orinoco, Uncle Hamish helped his niece settle the alligator comfortably in the wheelchair, packing it in with lots of wet cushions. The big sun bonnet nearly hid its snout, but Marilyn made it wear sunglasses to help the disguise.

'I shan't forget this,' Sir Hamish said in a deeply grateful voice.

'Neither shall I,' murmured Marilyn, wheeling the alligator out into the street.

As Marilyn pushed the disguised alligator through her front gate she noticed Archie Lightfoot pushing a large motorized wheelchair through his front gate, too. Sitting in it was someone muffled in a scarf, a floppy hat and sunglasses.

'My old grandfather is coming to live with me for a while,' Archie said with a nervous laugh.

'How funny!' said Marilyn. 'My old granny is coming to stay with *me*.'

The two old grandparents looked at each other through their sunglasses and grinned toothily.

'Unfortunately,' Archie added quickly, 'my old grandfather can sometimes be very crabby. He has a big heart, but occasionally he works himself up into a bad temper. Do warn your grandmother not to talk to him.'

'I have the same problem with Granny,' Marilyn replied. 'She is basically big-hearted, but at times she can be bad-tempered. If you try to talk to her when she's hungry, she just snaps your head off!'

At first, things went smoothly. Every day Marilyn gave the alligator a large breakfast of fish and tomato sauce. Then she tucked the huge reptile into the wheelchair with blankets soaked in home-made mud. Next, she wheeled it into the garden and settled it down with a bottle of cordial, an open tin of sardines and the newspaper. The alligator always looked eagerly over the fence to see what was going on next door.

In his garden, Archie Lightfoot was settling his old grandfather down with tuna-fish sandwiches and a motoring magazine. His

grandfather blew a daring kiss to Marilyn
Hawthorn's grandmother. Marilyn
saw her alligator blow one back.

'You are not to blow kisses to
a respectable old gentleman,' she
said sternly. The grandfather
blew another kiss and the
alligator did the same. Marilyn
smacked its paw. It tried to bite
her, but she was much too quick
for it.

While Marilyn Hawthorn and
Archie Lightfoot were at work, the two old
grandparents blew kisses to one another and tossed fishy snacks
across the fence.

That evening, when Marilyn Hawthorn got home, she noticed
that her alligator seemed rather ill. It sighed a great deal, and
merely toyed with its sardines at supper. Marilyn felt its forehead. It
was warm and feverish, a bad thing in alligators, which are, of
course, cold-blooded. She took it to the vet at once.

'What on earth is this?' cried the vet, listening to the alligator's
heart. 'This alligator is in love!'

The alligator sighed so deeply it accidentally swallowed the vet's
thermometer.

'It must be homesick for the Orinoco,' Marilyn thought to
herself. So she took a day off work, wrapped cool mud-packs
around the alligator, and put it in the marigold garden – with a large
photograph of the Orinoco river to look at.

As she was doing this, Archie Lightfoot's face appeared over the garden fence.

'Oh, I'm so worried about my grandfather,' he cried. 'I have had to take him to the vet − I mean, the doctor − and he sighed so deeply that he swallowed a stethoscope.'

'And I've had to take the day off work to look after my old granny,' said Marilyn. 'She has swallowed a thermometer.'

'Ahem!' coughed Archie Lightfoot, clearing his throat nervously. 'Perhaps, since you are taking the day off work, you might like to slip over and see my stamp collection.'

'I'd love to,' replied Marilyn.

Marilyn Hawthorn and Archie Lightfoot spent rather a long time looking at the stamp collection. They forgot their responsibilities. But when they switched on the radio, they were alarmed to hear the following announcement:

> 'We interrupt this programme to bring you horrifying news. Two twenty-foot saurians − crocodiles, or perhaps they are alligators − both wearing sunglasses, are driving down the main road in motorized wheelchairs.'

'Oh, no!' cried Archie Lightfoot.

'Oh, no!' cried Marilyn Hawthorn.

Together, they ran outside. Their two lawns were quite empty.

'This is serious,' gasped Marilyn. 'Oh, Mr Lightfoot, I must confess that my grandmother is really an alligator!'

'And my old grandfather's a crocodile,' cried Archie. 'I didn't dream that a lovely woman like you could be fond of reptiles.'

'We can discuss that later,' said Marilyn briskly. 'First, we must get our dear pets back.'

Quickly, they climbed into Marilyn's sports car and took off after the runaway reptiles. They soon saw them whizzing along in their wheelchairs. Overhead, a police helicopter hovered, with several policemen and the vet inside it.

'It's very strange,' said Marilyn, 'but they seem to be heading for my uncle's house. I do wish Uncle Hamish were at home. He would know what to do in a case like this.'

The runaways turned into the street where Marilyn's uncle lived, but they did not turn in at his gate. Instead, they went through the next-door gateway, straight to the home of the Reverend Crabtree.

Imagine Marilyn's surprise when she saw her Uncle Hamish sitting on the veranda, showing the Reverend Crabtree his souvenirs of the Orinoco.

'Uncle, I didn't know you were back!' she exclaimed.

'Well, I have only just returned,' he said, looking in amazement at the two reptiles. 'The Orinoco wasn't as good as I remembered it, so I came home early. But Marilyn, why has my alligator split itself in two?'

'Oh, Uncle, this is not another alligator – it's a crocodile. And it belongs to Archie Lightfoot,' Marilyn explained. 'These two bad reptiles ran away together in their wheelchairs and came here.'

By now the police helicopter had landed on the lawn, and the policemen, followed by the vet, came running over.

'Don't hurt those saurians,' the vet was shouting. 'They are not very well. They are in love!'

'Ah,' said the Reverend Crabtree. 'I understand! They have

eloped and wish to get married.'

The crocodile and the alligator swished their tails and snapped their jaws as one reptile, to show he was right.

'I'm not sure if I, a minister of the church, should marry an alligator and a crocodile,' said the Reverend Crabtree doubtfully. 'It doesn't seem very respectable.'

'But it seems a pity to miss out on the chance of marrying two creatures so clearly in love,' said Archie. Then, turning to Marilyn, he added, 'Suppose we get married, too. Will that make it more respectable? After all, we did bring these two reptiles together. It's only fair that they should do the same for us!'

So Marilyn Hawthorn married Archie Lightfoot, and the crocodile and alligator were married too. Sir Hamish gave both brides away. Then he swapped over and became best man to the two bridegrooms.

Marilyn and Archie turned their two little houses into one large house, and their lawns into a swimming-pool for the two saurians. And they lived happily ever after, even though they had to begin every morning of their lives together feeding sardines to a handsome Nile crocodile and an Orinoco alligator – both with big hearts and even bigger appetites.

Rudyard Kipling

JUST SO STORIES

ILLUSTRATED BY MIKE TERRY

HOW THE CAMEL GOT HIS HUMP

NOW this is the next tale, and it tells how the Camel got his big hump.

In the beginning of years, when the world was so new-and-all, and the Animals were just beginning to work for Man, there was a Camel, and he lived in the middle of a Howling Desert because he did not want to work; and besides, he was a Howler himself. So he ate sticks and thorns and tamarisks and milkweed and prickles, most 'scruciating idle; and when anybody spoke to him he said, 'Humph!' Just 'Humph!' and no more.

Presently the Horse came to him on Monday morning, with a saddle on his back and a bit in his mouth, and said, 'Camel, O Camel, come out and trot like the rest of us.'

'Humph!' said the Camel; and the Horse went away and told the Man.

Presently the Dog came to him, with a stick in his mouth, and said, 'Camel, O Camel, come and fetch and carry like the rest of us.'

'Humph!' said the Camel; and the Dog went away and told the Man.

Presently the Ox came to him, with the yoke on his neck, and said, 'Camel, O Camel, come and plough like the rest of us.'

'Humph!' said the Camel; and the Ox went away and told the Man.

At the end of the day the Man called the Horse and the Dog and the Ox together, and said, 'Three, O Three, I'm very sorry for you (with the world so new-and-all); but that Humph-thing in the Desert can't work, or he would have been here by now, so I am going to leave him alone, and you must work double-time to make up for it.'

That made the Three very angry (with the world so new-and-all), and they held a palaver, and an *indaba*, and a *punchayet*, and a pow-wow on the edge of the Desert; and the Camel came chewing milkweed *most* 'scruciating idle, and laughed at them. Then he said 'Humph!' and went away again.

Presently there came along the Djinn in charge of All Deserts, rolling in a cloud of dust (Djinns always travel that way because it is Magic), and he stopped to palaver and pow-wow with the Three.

'Djinn of All Deserts,' said the Horse, 'is it right for any one to be idle, with the world so new-and-all?'

'Certainly not,' said the Djinn.

'Well,' said the Horse, 'there's a thing in the middle of your Howling Desert (and he's a Howler himself) with a long neck and long legs, and he hasn't done a stroke of work since Monday morning. He won't trot.'

'Whew!' said the Djinn, whistling, 'that's my Camel, for all the gold in Arabia! What does he say about it?'

'He says "Humph!"' said the Dog; 'and he won't fetch and carry.'

'Does he say anything else?'

'Only "Humph!"; and he won't plough,' said the Ox.

'Very good,' said the Djinn. 'I'll humph him if you will kindly wait a minute.'

The Djinn rolled himself up in his dustcloak, and took a bearing across the desert, and found the Camel most 'scruciatingly idle, looking at his own reflection in a pool of water.

'My long and bubbling friend,' said the Djinn, 'what's this I hear of your doing no work, with the world so new-and-all?'

'Humph!' said the Camel.

The Djinn sat down, with his chin in his hand, and began to think a Great Magic, while the Camel looked at his own reflection in the pool of water.

'You've given the Three extra work ever since Monday morning, all on account of your 'scruciating idleness,' said the Djinn; and he went on thinking Magics, with his chin in his hand.

'Humph!' said the Camel.

'I shouldn't say that again if I were you,' said the Djinn; 'you might say it once too often. Bubbles, I want you to work.'

And the Camel said 'Humph!' again; but no sooner had he said it than he saw his back, that he was so proud of, puffing up and

puffing up into a great big lolloping humph.

'Do you see that?' said the Djinn. 'That's your very own humph that you've brought upon your very own self by not working. Today is Thursday, and you've done no work since Monday, when the work began. Now you are going to work.'

'How can I,' said the Camel, 'with this humph on my back?'

'That's made a-purpose,' said the Djinn, 'all because you missed those three days. You will be able to work now for three days without eating, because you can live on your humph; and don't you ever say I never did anything for you. Come out of the Desert and go to the Three, and behave. Humph yourself!'

And the Camel humphed himself, humph and all, and went away to join the Three. And from that day to this the Camel always wears a humph (we call it 'hump' now, not to hurt his feelings); but he has never yet caught up with the three days that he missed at the beginning of the world, and he has never yet learned how to behave.

Louisa May Alcott

LITTLE WOMEN

ILLUSTRATED BY EMMA CHICHESTER CLARK

JO MEETS APOLLYON

The four March girls, Meg, Jo, Beth and Amy, are growing up at the time
of the American Civil War. Although their father is away with the army
and they are quite poor, they are a happy family. But in this extract Jo
and Amy have a really dreadful quarrel.

'GIRLS, where are you going?' asked Amy, coming into
their room one Saturday afternoon, and finding them
getting ready to go out, with an air of secrecy, which
excited her curiosity.

'Never mind; little girls shouldn't ask questions,' returned Jo,
sharply.

Now if there *is* anything mortifying to our feelings, when we are
young, it is to be told that; and to be bidden to 'run away, dear', is
still more trying to us. Amy bridled up at this insult, and determined
to find out the secret, if she teased for an hour. Turning to Meg, who
never refused her anything very long, she said coaxingly, 'Do tell me!

I should think you might let me go too; for Beth is fussing over her piano, and I haven't got anything to do, and am *so* lonely.'

'I can't, dear, because you aren't invited,' began Meg; but Jo broke in impatiently, 'Now, Meg, be quiet, or you will spoil it all. You can't go, Amy; so don't be a baby and whine about it.'

'You are going somewhere with Laurie, I know you are; you were whispering and laughing together, on the sofa, last night, and you stopped when I came in. Aren't you going with him?'

'Yes, we are; now do be still and stop bothering.'

Amy held her tongue, but used her eyes, and saw Meg slip a fan into her pocket.

'I know! I know! You're going to the hall to see "The Seven Castles"!' she cried, adding resolutely, 'and I *shall* go, for Mother said I might see it; and I've got my rag-money, and it was mean not to tell me in time.'

'Just listen to me a minute, and be a good child,' said Meg, soothingly. 'Mother doesn't wish you to go this week, because your eyes are not well enough yet to bear the light of this fairy piece. Next week you can go with Beth and Hannah, and have a nice time.'

'I don't like that half as well as going with you and Laurie. Please let me; I've been sick with this cold for so long, and shut up, I'm dying for some fun. Do, Meg! I'll be ever so good,' pleaded Amy, looking as pathetic as she could.

'Suppose we take her. I don't believe Mother would mind, if we bundle her up well,' began Meg.

'If *she* goes *I* shan't; and if I don't, Laurie won't like it; and it will be very rude, after he invited only us, to go and drag in Amy. I

should think she'd hate to poke herself where she isn't wanted,' said Jo, crossly, for she disliked the trouble of overseeing a fidgety child, when she wanted to enjoy herself.

Her tone and manner angered Amy, who began to put her boots on, saying, in her most aggravating way, 'I *shall* go; Meg says I may; and if I pay for myself, Laurie hasn't anything to do with it.'

'You can't sit with us, for our seats are reserved, and you mustn't sit alone; so Laurie will give you his place, and that will spoil our pleasure; or he'll get another seat for you, and that isn't proper, when you weren't asked. You shan't stir a step; so you may just have to stay where you are,' scolded Jo, crosser than ever, having just pricked her finger in her hurry.

Sitting on the floor, with one boot on, Amy began to cry, and

Meg to reason with her, when Laurie called from below, and the two girls hurried down, leaving their sister wailing; for now and then she forgot her grown-up ways, and acted like a spoilt child. Just as the party were setting out, Amy called over the banisters, in a threatening voice, 'You'll be sorry for this, Jo March; see if you ain't.'

'Fiddlesticks!' returned Jo, slamming the door.

They had a charming time, for 'The Seven Castles of the Diamond Lake' was as brilliant and wonderful as heart could wish. But, in spite of the comical red imps, sparkling elves, and gorgeous princes and princesses, Jo's pleasure had a drop of bitterness in it; the fairy queen's yellow curls reminded her of Amy; and between the acts she amused herself with wondering what her sister would do to make her 'sorry for it'. She and Amy had had many lively skirmishes in the course of their lives, for both had quick tempers, and were apt to be violent when fairly roused. Amy teased Jo, Jo irritated Amy, and semi-occasional explosions occurred, of which both were much ashamed afterwards. Although the oldest, Jo had the least self-control, and had hard times trying to curb the fiery spirit which was continually getting her into trouble; her anger never lasted long, and having humbly confessed her fault she sincerely repented and tried to do better. Her sisters used to say that they rather liked to get Jo into a fury because she was such an angel afterwards. Poor Jo tried desperately to be good, but her bosom enemy was always ready to flame up and defeat her; and it took years of patient effort to subdue it.

When they got home they found Amy reading in the parlour. She assumed an injured air as they came in; never lifted her eyes from her book, or asked a single question. Perhaps curiosity might have conquered resentment, if Beth had not been there to inquire, and receive a glowing description of the play. On going up to put away her best hat, Jo's first look was towards the bureau; for, in their last quarrel, Amy had soothed her feelings by turning Jo's top drawer upside down on the floor. Everything was in its place, however, and after a hasty glance into her various closets, bags, and boxes, Jo decided that Amy had forgiven and forgotten her wrongs.

There Jo was mistaken; for next day she made a discovery which produced a tempest. Meg, Beth, and Amy were sitting together, late in the afternoon, when Jo burst into the room, looking excited, and demanding breathlessly, 'Has anyone taken my book?'

Meg and Beth said 'No,' at once, and looked surprised; Amy poked the fire, and said nothing. Jo saw her colour rise, and was down upon her in a minute.

'Amy, you've got it.'

'No, I haven't.'

'You know where it is, then!'

'No, I don't.'

'That's a fib!' cried Jo, taking her by the shoulders and looking fierce enough to frighten a much braver child than Amy.

'It isn't. I haven't got it, don't know where it is now, and don't care.'

'You know something about it, and you'd better tell at once, or I'll make you,' and Jo gave her a slight shake.

'Scold as much as you like, you'll never see your silly old book again,' cried Amy, getting excited in her turn.

'Why not?'

'I burnt it up.'

'What! My little book I was so fond of, and worked over, and meant to finish before Father got home! Have you really burnt it?' said Jo, turning very pale, while her eyes kindled and her hands clutched Amy nervously.

'Yes, I did! I told you I'd make you pay for being so cross yesterday, and I have, so —'

Amy got no further, for Jo's hot temper mastered her, and she shook Amy till her teeth chattered in her head; crying in a passion of grief and anger:

'You wicked, wicked girl! I never can write it again and I'll never forgive you as long as I live.'

Meg flew to rescue Amy, and Beth to pacify Jo, but Jo was quite beside herself; and with a parting box on her sister's ear, she rushed out of the room up to the old sofa in the garret, and finished her fight alone.

The storm cleared up below, for Mrs March came home, and, having heard the story, soon brought Amy to a sense of the wrong she had done her sister. Jo's book was the pride of her heart, and was regarded by her family as a literary sprout of great promise. It was only half a dozen little fairy tales, but Jo had worked over them patiently, putting her whole heart into her work hoping to make something good enough to print. She had just copied them with great care, and had destroyed the old manuscript, so that Amy's bonfire had consumed the loving work of several years. It seemed a small loss to others, but to Jo it was a dreadful calamity, and she felt that it never could be made up to her. Beth mourned as for a departed kitten, and Meg refused to defend her pet; Mrs March looked grave and grieved, and Amy felt that no one would love her till she had asked pardon for the act which she now regretted more than any of them.

When the tea-bell rang Jo appeared, looking so grim and unapproachable, that it took all Amy's courage to say meekly:

'Please forgive me, Jo; I'm very, very sorry.'

'I never shall forgive you,' was Jo's stern answer; and from that moment she ignored Amy entirely.

No one spoke of the great trouble – not even Mrs March – for all had learned by experience that when Jo was in that mood words were wasted; and the wisest course was to wait till some little accident, or her own generous nature, softened Jo's resentment, and healed the breach. It was not a happy evening; for though they sewed as usual, while their mother read aloud from Bremer, Scott, or Edgeworth, something was wanting and the sweet home peace was disturbed. They felt this most when singing time came; for Beth could only play, Jo stood dumb as stone, and Amy broke down, so Meg and Mother sang alone. But in spite of their efforts to be as cheery as larks, the flute-like voices did not seem to chord as well as usual, and all felt out of tune.

As Jo received her good-night kiss, Mrs March whispered gently: 'My dear, don't let the sun go down upon your anger; forgive each other, help each other, and begin again tomorrow.'

Jo wanted to lay her head down on that motherly bosom, and cry her grief and anger all away, but tears were an unmanly weakness, and she felt so deeply injured that she really *couldn't* quite forgive yet. So she winked hard, shook her head, and said gruffly, because Amy was listening: 'It was an abominable thing, and she don't deserve to be forgiven.'

With that she marched off to bed, and there was no merry or confidential gossip that night.

T. H. White

THE ONCE AND FUTURE KING

ILLUSTRATED BY PAULINE BAYNES

THE SWORD IN THE STONE

Merlyn the magician has taught the young King Arthur many things by turning him into different animals. Now Arthur, nicknamed the Wart, faces his first great trial.

L ONDON was full to the brim. If Sir Ector had not been lucky enough to own a little land in Pie Street, on which there stood a respectable inn, they would have been hard put to it to find a lodging. But he did own it, and as a matter of fact drew most of his dividends from that source, so they were able to get three beds between the five of them. They thought themselves fortunate.

On the first day of the tournament, Sir Kay managed to get them on the way to the lists at least an hour before the jousts could possibly begin. He had lain awake all night imagining how he was going to beat the best barons in England, and he had not been able to eat his breakfast. Now he rode at the front of the cavalcade, with pale cheeks, and the Wart wished there was something he could do to calm him down.

For country people, who only knew the dismantled tilting ground of Sir Ector's castle, the scene which met their eyes was ravishing. It was a huge green pit in the earth, about as big as the arena at a football match. It lay ten feet lower than the surrounding country, with sloping banks, and the snow had been swept off it. It had been kept warm with straw, which had been cleared off that morning, and now the close-worn grass sparkled green in the white landscape. Round the arena there was a world of colour so dazzling and moving and twinkling as to make one blink one's eyes. The wooden grandstands were painted in scarlet and white. The silk

pavilions of famous people, pitched on every side, were azure and green and saffron and chequered. The pennons and pennoncels which floated everywhere in the sharp wind were flapping with every colour of the rainbow, as they strained and slapped at their flag-poles, and the barrier down the middle of the arena itself was done in chessboard squares of black and white. Most of the combatants and their friends had not yet arrived, but one could see from those few who had come how the very people would turn the scene into a bank of flowers, and how the armour would flash, and the scalloped sleeves of the heralds jig in the wind, as they raised their brazen trumpets to their lips to shake the fleecy clouds of winter with joyances and fanfares.

'Good heavens!' cried Sir Kay. 'I have left my sword at home.'

'Can't joust without a sword,' said Sir Grummore. 'Quite irregular.'

'Better go and fetch it,' said Sir Ector. 'You have time.'

'My squire will do it,' said Sir Kay. 'What a damned mistake to make! Here, squire, ride hard back to the inn and fetch my sword. You shall have a shilling if you fetch it in time.'

The Wart went as pale as Sir Kay was, and looked as if he were going to strike him. Then he said, 'It shall be done, master,' and turned his ambling palfrey against the stream of newcomers. He began to push his way towards their hostelry as best he might.

'To offer me money!' cried the Wart to himself. 'To look down at this beastly little donkey-affair off his great charger and to call me Squire! Oh, Merlyn, give me patience with the brute, and stop me from throwing his filthy shilling in his face.'

When he got to the inn it was closed. Everybody had thronged to see the famous tournament, and the entire household had followed after the mob. Those were lawless days and it was not safe to leave your house – or even to go to sleep in it – unless you were certain that it was impregnable. The wooden shutters bolted over the downstairs windows were two inches thick, and the doors were double-barred.

'Now what do I do,' asked the Wart, 'to earn my shilling?'

He looked ruefully at the blind little inn, and began to laugh.

'Poor Kay,' he said. 'All that shilling stuff was only because he was scared and miserable, and now he has good cause to be. Well, he shall have a sword of some sort if I have to break into the Tower of London.

'How does one get hold of a sword?' he continued. 'Where can I steal one? Could I waylay some knight, even if I am mounted on an ambling pad, and take his weapon by force? There must be some swordsmith or armourer in a great town like this, whose shop would be still open.'

He turned his mount and cantered off down the street. There was a quiet churchyard at the end of it, with a kind of square in front of the church door. In the middle of the square there was a heavy stone with an anvil on it, and a fine new sword was stuck through the anvil.

'Well,' said the Wart, 'I suppose it is some sort of war memorial, but it will have to do. I am sure nobody would grudge Kay a war memorial, if they knew his desperate straits.'

He tied his reins round a post of the lych-gate, strode up the gravel path, and took hold of the sword.

'Come, sword,' he said. 'I must cry your mercy and take you for a better cause.

'This is extraordinary,' said the Wart. 'I feel strange when I have hold of this sword, and I notice everything much more clearly. Look at the beautiful gargoyles of the church, and of the monastery which it belongs to. See how splendidly all the famous banners in the aisle are waving. How nobly that yew holds up the red flakes of its timbers to worship God. How clean the snow is. I can smell something like feverfew and sweet briar – and is it music that I hear?'

It was music, whether of pan-pipes or of recorders, and the light in the churchyard was so clear, without being dazzling, that one could have picked a pin out twenty yards away.

'There is something in this place,' said the Wart. 'There are people. Oh, people, what do you want?'

Nobody answered him, but the music was loud and the light beautiful.

'People,' cried the Wart, 'I must take this sword. It is not for me, but for Kay. I will bring it back.'

There was still no answer, and the Wart turned back to the anvil. He saw the golden letters, which he did not read, and the jewels on the pommel, flashing in the lovely light.

'Come, sword,' said the Wart. He took hold of the handles with both hands, and strained against the stone. There was a melodious consort on the recorders, but nothing moved.

The Wart let go of the handles, when they were beginning to bite into the palms of his hands, and stepped back, seeing stars.

'It is well fixed,' he said.

He took hold of it again and pulled with all his might. The music played more strongly, and the light all about the churchyard glowed like amethysts; but the sword still stuck.

'Oh, Merlyn,' cried the Wart, 'help me to get this weapon.'

There was a kind of rushing noise, and a long chord played along with it. All round the churchyard there were hundreds of old friends. They rose over the church wall all together, like the Punch and Judy ghosts of remembered days, and there were badgers and nightingales and vulgar crows and hares and wild geese and falcons and fishes and

dogs and dainty unicorns and solitary wasps and corkindrills and hedgehogs and griffins and the thousand other animals he had met. They loomed round the church wall, the lovers and helpers of the Wart, and they all spoke solemnly in turn. Some of them had come from the banners in the church, where they were painted in heraldry, some from the waters and the sky and the fields about – but all, down to the smallest shrew mouse, had come to help on account of love. The Wart felt his power grow.

'Put your back into it,' said a Luce (or pike) off one of the heraldic banners, 'as you once did when I was going to snap you up. Remember that power springs from the nape of the neck.'

'What about those forearms,' asked a badger gravely, 'that are held together by a chest? Come along, my dear embryo, and find your tool.'

A Merlin sitting at the top of the yew tree cried out, 'Now then, Captain Wart, what is the first law of the foot? I thought I once heard something about never letting go?'

'Don't work like a stalling woodpecker,' urged a Tawny Owl affectionately. 'Keep up a steady effort, my duck, and you will have it yet.'

A white-front said, 'Now, Wart, if you were once able to fly the great North Sea, surely you can co-ordinate a few little wing-muscles here and there? Fold your powers together, with the spirit of your mind, and it will come out like butter. Come along, Homo sapiens, for all we humble friends of yours are waiting here to cheer.'

The Wart walked up to the great sword for the third time. He put out his right hand softly and drew it out as gently as from a scabbard.

∾

Joan Aiken

HUMBLEPUPPY

ILLUSTRATED BY TONY ROSS

OUR house was furnished mainly from auction sales. When you buy furniture that way you get a lot of extra things besides the particular piece that you were after, because the stuff is sold in lots: *Lot 13, two Persian rugs, a set of golf-clubs, a sewing-machine, a walnut radio-cabinet, and a plinth.*

It was in this way that I acquired a tin deedbox, which came with two coal-scuttles and a broom cupboard. The deedbox is solid metal, painted black, big as a medium-sized suitcase. When I first brought it home I put it in my study, planning to use it as a kind of filing-cabinet for old typescripts. I had gone into the kitchen, and was arranging the brooms in their new home, when I heard a muffled thumping coming from the study. I went back, thinking that a bird must have flown in through the window; no bird, but the thumping seemed to be inside

the deedbox. I had already opened it to see if there were any diamonds or bearer bonds worth thousands of pounds inside (there weren't), but now I opened it again. The key was attached to the handle by a thin chain. There was nothing inside. I shut it. The noise started again. I opened it. Still nothing inside.

Well, this was broad daylight, two o'clock on Thursday afternoon, people going past in the road outside and a radio schools programme chatting away to itself in the next room. It was not a ghostly kind of time, so I put my hand into the empty box and moved it about.

Something shrank away from my hand. I heard a faint, scared whimper. It could almost have been my own, but wasn't. Knowing that someone – something? – else was afraid too put heart into me. Exploring carefully and gently around the interior of the box, I felt the contour of a small, bony, warm, trembling body with big awkward feet, silky dangling ears, and a cold nose that, when I found it, nudged for a moment anxiously but trustingly into the palm of my hand.

So I knelt down, put the other hand into the box as well, cupped them under a thin little ribby chest, and lifted out – Humblepuppy. He was quite light.

I couldn't see him, but I could hear his faint inquiring whimper, and I could hear his toenails scratching on the floorboards.

Just at that moment the cat, Taffy, came in.

Taffy has a lot of character. Every cat has a lot of character, but Taffy has more than most, all of it inconvenient. For instance, although he is very sociable, and longs for company, he just despises company in the form of dogs. The mere sound of a dog

47

barking two streets away is enough to make his fur stand up like a porcupine's quills and his tail swell like a mushroom cloud.

Which it did the instant he saw Humblepuppy.

Now here is the interesting thing. *I* could feel and hear Humblepuppy, but couldn't see him; *Taffy*, apparently, could see and smell him, but couldn't feel him. We soon discovered this. For Taffy, sinking into a low, gladiatorial crouch, letting out all the time a fearsome throaty wailing, like a bagpipe revving up its drone, inched his way along to where Humblepuppy huddled trembling by my left foot, and then dealt him what ought to have been a swinging right-handed clip on the ear. 'Get out of my house, you filthy little canine scum!' was what he was plainly intending to convey.

But the swipe failed to connect; instead it landed on my shin.

I've never seen a cat so astonished. It was like watching a kitten meet itself for the first time in a looking-glass. Taffy ran round to the back of where Humblepuppy was sitting; felt; smelt; poked gingerly

with a paw; leapt back nervously; crept forward again. All the
time Humblepuppy just sat, trembling a little, giving out this faint
beseeching sound that meant: 'I'm only a poor little mongrel
without a smidgeon of harm in me. *Please* don't do anything nasty!
I don't even know how I came here.'

It certainly was a puzzle how he had come. I rang the
auctioneers (after shutting Taffy *out* and Humblepuppy *into* the
study with a bowl of water and a handful of Boniebisk, Taffy's
favourite breakfast food).

The auctioneers told me that *Lot 12, Deedbox, coal-scuttles and
broom cupboard*, had come from Riverland Rectory, where Mr
Smythe, the old rector, had lately died aged ninety. Had he ever
possessed a dog, or a puppy? They couldn't say; they had merely
received instructions from a firm of lawyers to sell the furniture.

I never did discover how poor little Humblepuppy's ghost got
into that deedbox. Maybe he was shut in by mistake, long ago;

maybe some callous Victorian gardener dropped him, box and all, into a river, and the box was later found.

Anyway, and whatever had happened in the past, now that Humblepuppy had come out of his box he was very ready to be grateful and affectionate. As I sat typing I'd often hear a patter-patter, and feel his small chin fit itself comfortably over my foot, ears dangling. Goodness knows what kind of a mixture he was; something between a spaniel and a terrier, I'd guess. In the evening, watching television or sitting by the fire, one would suddenly find his warm weight leaning against one's leg. (He didn't put on a lot of weight, but his bony little ribs filled out a bit.)

For the first few weeks we had a lot of trouble with Taffy, who was very surly over the whole business and blamed me bitterly for not getting rid of this low-class intruder. But Humblepuppy was extremely placating, got back into his deedbox whenever the atmosphere became too volcanic, and did his very best not to be a nuisance.

By and by Taffy thawed. As I've said, he is really a very sociable cat. Although quite old, seventy cat years, he dearly likes cheerful company, and generally has some young cat friend who comes to play with him. In the last few years we've had Whisky, the black-and-white pub cat, who used to sit washing the smell of fish-and-chips off his fur under the dripping tap in our kitchen sink; Tetanus, the hairdresser's thick-set black, who took a fancy to sleeping on top of our china cupboard every night, and used to startle me very much by jumping down heavily on to my shoulder as I made the breakfast coffee; Sweet Charity, a little grey Persian who came to a sad end under the wheels of a police car, and Charity's

grey-and-white stripy cousin Fred, whose owners presently moved from next door to another part of the town.

It was soon after Fred's departure that Humblepuppy arrived, and from my point of view he couldn't have been more welcome. Taffy missed Fred badly, and expected *me* to play with him instead; it was sad to see this large elderly tabby rushing hopefully up and down the stairs after breakfast, or hiding behind the armchair and jumping out on to nobody; or howling, howling, howling at me till I escorted him out into the garden where he'd rush to the lavender bush which had been the traditional hiding-place of Whisky, Tetanus, Charity, and Fred in succession.

So sometimes, on a working morning, I'd be at my wits' end, almost on the point of going across the town to our ex-neighbours, ringing the bell, and saying, 'Please can Fred come and play?'

Specially on a rainy, uninviting day, when Taffy was pacing gloomily about the house with drooping head and switching tail, grumbling about the weather and the lack of company, and blaming me for both. Humblepuppy's arrival changed all that.

At first Taffy considered it necessary to police him, and that kept him fully occupied for hours. He'd sit on guard by the deedbox till Humblepuppy woke up in the morning, and then he'd follow officiously all over the house. Humblepuppy was slow and cautious in his explorations, but by degrees he picked up courage and found his way into every corner. He never once made a puddle; he learned to use Taffy's cat-flap and go out into the garden, though he was always more timid outside and would scamper for home at any loud noise. Planes and cars terrified him, which made me still more certain that he had been in that deedbox for a long, long time, since before such things were invented.

Presently he learned, or Taffy taught him, to hide in the lavender bush like Whisky, Charity, Tetanus, and Fred; and the two of them used to play their own ghostly version of touch-last for hours on end.

When visitors came, Humblepuppy always retired to his deedbox; he was decidedly scared of strangers; which made his behaviour with Mr Manningham, the new rector of Riverland, all the more surprising.

As I was dying to learn anything I could of the old rectory's history, I'd invited Mr Manningham to tea. He was a thin, gentle, quiet man, who had done missionary work in the Far East and had fallen ill and had had to come back to England. He seemed a little sad and lonely. I liked him. He told me that for a large part of the nineteenth century the Riverland living had belonged to a parson called the Reverend Timothy Swannett, who had lived to a great age and had had ten children.

'He was a great-uncle of mine as a matter of fact. But why do you want to know all this?' Mr Manningham asked. His long thin arm hung over the side of his chair; absently he moved his hand sideways and remarked, 'I didn't know you had a puppy.' Then he looked down and said, 'Oh!'

'He's never come out for a stranger before,' I said.

Humblepuppy climbed invisibly on to Mr Manningham's lap.

We agreed that the new rector probably carried a familiar smell of his rectory with him, or possibly he reminded Humblepuppy of his great-uncle the Rev. Swannett. Anyway, after that, Humblepuppy always came scampering joyfully out if Mr Manningham dropped in to tea, so of course I thought of the rector when summer holiday time came round.

During the summer holiday we lend our house and cat to a lady publisher and her mother who are devoted to cats and think it a privilege to look after Taffy and spoil him. He is always amazingly overweight when we get back. But the old lady has an allergy to dogs, and is frightened of them too, so it was plainly out of the question that she should be expected to share her summer holiday with the ghost of a puppy.

So I asked Mr Manningham if he'd be prepared to take Humblepuppy as a boarder, since it didn't seem a case for the usual kind of boarding-kennels; he said he'd be delighted.

I drove Humblepuppy out to Riverland in his deedbox; he was rather miserable on the drive but luckily it is not far. Mr

Manningham came out into the garden to meet me. We put the box down on the lawn and opened it.

I've never heard a puppy so wildly excited. Often I'd been sorry that I couldn't see Humblepuppy, but I was never sorrier than on that afternoon, as we heard him rushing from tree to familiar tree, barking joyously, dashing through the orchard grass – you could see it divide as he whizzed along – coming back to bounce up against us, all damp and earthy and smelling of leaves.

'He's going to be happy with you all right,' I said, and Mr Manningham's grey, lined face crinkled into its thoughtful smile as he said, 'It's the place more than me, I think.' Well, it was both of them really.

When the holiday was over I went round to collect Humblepuppy, leaving Taffy haughty and standoffish, sniffing our cases. It always takes him a long time to forgive us for going away.

Mr Manningham had a bit of a cold and was sitting by the fire in his study, wrapped in a Shetland rug. Humblepuppy was on his knee. I could hear the little dog's tail thump against the arm of the chair when I walked in, but he didn't get down to greet me. He stayed in Mr Manningham's lap.

'So you've come to take back my boarder,' Mr Manningham said.

There was nothing in the least strained about his voice or smile but – I just hadn't the heart to take back Humblepuppy. I put my hand down, found his soft wrinkly forehead, rumpled it a bit, and said, 'Well – I was sort of wondering; our spoilt old cat seems to have got used to being on his own again and I was wondering whether – by any chance – you'd feel like keeping him?'

Mr Manningham's face lit up. He didn't speak for a minute, then he put a gentle hand down and rubbed a finger along Humblepuppy's chin.

'Well,' he said. He cleared his throat. 'Of course, if you're *quite* sure . . .'

'Quite sure.' My throat needed clearing too.

'I hope you won't catch my cold,' said Mr Manningham.

I shook my head and said, 'I'll drop in to see if you're better in a day or two,' and went off and left them together.

Poor Taffy was pretty glum over the loss of his playmate for several weeks; we had two hours' purgatory every morning after breakfast while he hunted for Humblepuppy high and low. But gradually the memory faded and, thank goodness, now he has found a new friend, Little Grey Furry, a nephew, cousin, or other relative of Charity and Fred. Little Grey Furry has learned to play hide-and-seek in the lavender bush, and to use our cat-flap, and clean up whatever's in Taffy's food bowl, so all is well in that department.

But I still miss Humblepuppy. I miss his cold nose exploring the palm of my hand as I sit thinking, in the middle of a page, and his warm weight leaning against my ankle as he watches the TV commercials. And the scritch-scratch of his toenails on the dining-room floor and the flump, flump as he comes downstairs, and the small hollow on a cushion as he settles down with a sigh.

Oh well. I'll get over it, just as Taffy has. But I was wondering about putting an ad into 'Our Dogs', or 'Pets' Monthly':

Wanted, ghost of mongrel puppy. Warm welcome, loving home.
Any reasonable price paid.

It might be worth a try.

L. Frank Baum

THE WIZARD OF OZ

ILLUSTRATED BY CHRIS RIDDELL

THE RESCUE OF THE TIN WOODMAN

Dorothy has been transported by a tornado from her farm in Kansas to Munchkinland. The only person who can tell her how to get home is the Wizard of Oz, who lives in the Emerald City. On her way to see him, Dorothy is joined by some strange companions.

WHEN Dorothy awoke the sun was shining through the trees and Toto had long been out chasing birds around her. There was the Scarecrow, still standing patiently in his corner, waiting for her.

'We must go and search for water,' she said to him.

'Why do you need water?' he asked.

'To wash my face clean after the dust of the road, and to drink, so the dry bread will not stick in my throat.'

'It must be inconvenient to be made of

flesh,' said the Scarecrow, thoughtfully, 'for you must sleep, and eat and drink. However, you have brains, and it is worth a lot of bother to be able to think properly.'

They left the cottage and walked through the trees until they found a little spring of clear water, where Dorothy drank and bathed and ate her breakfast. She saw there was not much bread left in the basket, and the girl was thankful the Scarecrow did not have to eat anything, for there was scarcely enough for herself and Toto for the day.

When she had finished her meal, and was about to go back to the road of yellow brick, she was startled to hear a deep groan near by.

'What was that?' she asked, timidly.

'I cannot imagine,' replied the Scarecrow; 'but we can go and see.'

Just then another groan reached their ears, and the sound seemed to come from behind them. They turned and walked through the forest a few steps, when Dorothy discovered something shining in a ray of sunshine that fell between the trees. She ran to the place and then stopped short, with a cry of surprise.

One of the big trees had been partly chopped through, and standing beside it, with an uplifted axe in his hands, was a man made entirely of tin. His head and arms and legs were jointed upon his body, but he stood perfectly motionless, as if he could not stir at all.

Dorothy looked at him in amazement, and so did the Scarecrow, while Toto barked sharply and made a snap at the tin legs, which hurt his teeth.

'Did you groan?' asked Dorothy.

'Yes,' answered the tin man, 'I did. I've been groaning for more than a year, and no one has ever heard me before or come to help me.'

'What can I do for you?' she inquired softly, for she was moved by the sad voice in which the man spoke.

'Get an oil-can and oil my joints,' he answered. 'They are rusted so badly that I cannot move them at all; if I am well oiled I shall soon be all right again. You will find an oil-can on a shelf in my cottage.'

Dorothy at once ran back to the cottage and found the oil-can, and then she returned and asked, anxiously, 'Where are your joints?'

'Oil my neck, first,' replied the Tin Woodman. So she oiled it, and as it was quite badly rusted the Scarecrow took hold of the tin head and moved it gently from side to side until it worked freely, and then the man could turn it himself.

'Now oil the joints in my arms,' he said. And Dorothy oiled them and the Scarecrow bent them carefully until they were quite free from rust and as good as new.

The Tin Woodman gave a sigh of satisfaction and lowered his axe, which he leaned against the tree.

'This is a great comfort,' he said. 'I have been holding that axe in the air ever since I rusted, and I'm glad to be able to put it down at last. Now, if you will oil the joints of my legs, I shall be all right once more.'

So they oiled his legs until he could move them freely; and he thanked them again and again for his release, for he seemed a very polite creature, and very grateful.

'I might have stood there always if you had not come along,' he

said; 'so you have certainly saved my life. How did you happen to be here?'

'We are on our way to the Emerald City, to see the great Oz,' she answered, 'and we stopped at your cottage to pass the night.'

'Why do you wish to see Oz?' he asked.

'I want him to send me back to Kansas; and the Scarecrow wants him to put a few brains into his head,' she replied.

The Tin Woodman appeared to think deeply for a moment. Then he said: 'Do you suppose Oz could give me a heart?'

'Why, I guess so,' Dorothy answered. 'It would be as easy as to give the Scarecrow brains.'

'True,' the Tin Woodman returned. 'So, if you will allow me to join your party, I will also go to the Emerald City and ask Oz to help me.'

'Come along,' said the Scarecrow heartily; and Dorothy added that she would be pleased to have his company. So the Tin Woodman shouldered his axe and they all passed through the forest until they came to the road that was paved with yellow brick.

The Tin Woodman had asked Dorothy to put the oil-can in her basket. 'For,' he said, 'if I should get caught in the rain, and rust again, I would need the oil-can badly.'

It was a bit of good luck to have their new comrade join the party, for soon after they had begun their journey again they came to a place where the trees and branches grew so thick over the road that the travellers could not pass. But the Tin Woodman set to work with his axe and chopped so well that soon he cleared a passage for the entire party.

Dorothy was thinking so earnestly as they walked along that she did not notice when the Scarecrow stumbled into a hole and rolled over to the side of the road. Indeed he was obliged to call to her to help him up again.

'Why didn't you walk around the hole?' asked the Tin Woodman.

'I don't know enough,' replied the Scarecrow cheerfully. 'My head is stuffed with straw, you know, and that is why I am going to Oz to ask him for some brains.'

'Oh, I see,' said the Tin Woodman. 'But, after all, brains are not the best things in the world.'

'Have you any?' inquired the Scarecrow.

'No, my head is quite empty,' answered the Woodman; 'but once I had brains, and a heart also; so, having tried them both, I should much rather have a heart.'

'And why is that?' asked the Scarecrow.

'I will tell you my story, and then you will know.'

So, while they were walking through the forest, the Tin Woodman told the following story:

'I was born the son of a woodman who chopped down trees in the forest and sold the wood for a living. When I grew up I too became a woodchopper, and after my father died I took care of my old mother as long as she lived. Then I made up my mind that instead of living alone I would marry, so that I might not become lonely.

'There was one of the Munchkin girls who was so beautiful that I soon grew to love her with all my heart. She, on her part, promised to marry me as soon as I could earn enough money to build a better house for her; so I set to work harder than ever. But the girl lived with an old woman who did not want her to marry anyone, for she was so lazy she wished the girl to remain with her and do

the cooking and the housework. So the old woman went to the Wicked Witch of the East, and promised her two sheep and a cow if she would prevent the marriage. Thereupon the Wicked Witch enchanted my axe, and when I was chopping away at my best one day, for I was anxious to get the new house and my wife as soon as possible, the axe slipped all at once and cut off my left leg.

'This at first seemed a great misfortune, for I knew a one-legged man could not do very well as a woodchopper. So I went to a tinsmith and had him make me a new leg out of tin. The leg worked very well, once I was used to it; but my action angered the Wicked Witch of the East, for she had promised the old woman I should not marry the pretty Munchkin girl. When I began chopping again my axe slipped and cut off my right leg. Again I went to the tinner, and again he made me a leg out of tin. After this the enchanted axe cut off my arms, one after the other; but, nothing daunted, I had them replaced with tin ones. The Wicked Witch then made the axe slip and cut off my head, and at first I thought that was the end of me. But the tinsmith happened to come along, and he made me a new head out of tin.

'I thought I had beaten the Wicked Witch then, and I worked harder than ever; but I little knew how cruel my enemy could be. She thought of a new way to kill my love for the beautiful Munchkin maiden, and made my axe slip again, so that it cut right through my body, splitting me into two halves. Once more the tinsmith came to my help and made me a body of tin, fastening my tin arms and legs and head to it, by means of joints, so that I could move around as well as ever. But, alas! I had now no heart, so that I lost all my love for the Munchkin girl, and did not care whether I married her or not. I suppose she is still living with the old woman, waiting for me to come after her.

'My body shone so brightly in the sun that I felt very proud of it and it did not matter now if my axe slipped, for it could not cut me. There was only one danger – that my joints would rust; but I kept an oil-can in my cottage and took care to oil myself whenever I needed it. However, there came a day when I forgot to do this, and, being caught in a rainstorm, before I thought of the danger my joints had rusted, and I was left to stand in the woods until you came to help me. It was a terrible thing to undergo, but during the year I stood there I had time to think that the greatest loss I had known was the loss of my heart. While I was in love I was the happiest man on earth; but no one can love who has not a heart, and so I am resolved to ask Oz to give me one. If he does, I will go back to the Munchkin maiden and marry her.'

Both Dorothy and the Scarecrow had been greatly interested in the story of the Tin Woodman, and now they knew why he was so anxious to get a new heart.

'All the same,' said the Scarecrow, 'I shall ask for brains instead of a heart; for a fool would not know what to do with a heart if he had one.'

'I shall take the heart,' returned the Tin Woodman, 'for brains do not make one happy, and happiness is the best thing in the world.'

E. Nesbit

THE RAILWAY CHILDREN

ILLUSTRATED BY ROBIN BELL CORFIELD

THE END

When Father goes away unexpectedly, Roberta, Peter, Phyllis and their
mother have to leave their old home to live in a small cottage near a
country railway station. They soon make new friends at the Railway, but
no one can tell them where Father is, or when he will return.
Then one day . . .

'I WISH something would happen,' said Bobbie, dreamily, 'something wonderful.'

And something wonderful did happen exactly four days after she had said this. I wish I could say it was three days after, because in fairy tales it is always three days after that things happen. But this is not a fairy story, and besides, it really was four and not three, and I am nothing if not strictly truthful.

They seemed to be hardly Railway children at all in those days,

and as the days went on each had an uneasy feeling about this which Phyllis expressed one day.

'I wonder if the Railway misses us,' she said, plaintively. 'We never go to see it now.'

'It seems ungrateful,' said Bobbie; 'we loved it so when we hadn't anyone to play with.'

'Perks is always coming up to ask after Jim,' said Peter, 'and the signalman's little boy is better. He told me so.'

'I didn't mean the people,' explained Phyllis; 'I meant the dear Railway itself.'

'The thing I don't like,' said Bobbie, on this fourth day, which was a Tuesday, 'is having stopped waving to the 9.15 and sending our love to Father by it.'

'Let's begin again,' said Phyllis. And they did.

Somehow the change of everything that was made by having servants in the house and Mother not doing any writing made the time seem extremely long since that strange morning at the beginning of things, when they had got up so early and burnt the bottom out of the kettle and had apple pie for breakfast and first seen the Railway.

It was September now, and the turf on the slope to the Railway was dry and crisp. Little long grass spikes stood up like bits of gold wire, frail blue harebells trembled on their tough, slender stalks. Gipsy roses opened wide and flat their lilac-coloured discs, and the golden stars of St John's Wort shone at the edges of the pool that lay half-way to the Railway. Bobbie gathered a generous handful of the flowers and thought how pretty they would look lying on the green-and-pink blanket of silk waste that now covered Jim's poor broken leg.

'Hurry up,' said Peter, 'or we shall miss the 9.15!'

'I can't hurry more than I am doing,' said Phyllis. 'Oh, bother it! My bootlace has come undone *again*!'

'When you're married,' said Peter, 'your bootlace will come undone going up the church aisle, and your man that you're going to get married to will tumble over it and smash his nose in on the ornamented pavement; and then you'll say you won't marry him, and you'll have to be an old maid.'

'I shan't,' said Phyllis. 'I'd much rather marry a man with his nose smashed in than not marry anybody.'

'It would be horrid to marry a man with a smashed nose all the same,' went on Bobbie. 'He wouldn't be able to smell the flowers at the wedding. Wouldn't that be awful!'

'Bother the flowers at the wedding!' cried Peter. 'Look! The signal's down. We must run!'

They ran. And once more they waved their handkerchiefs without at all minding whether the handkerchiefs were clean or not, to the 9.15.

'Take our love to Father!' cried Bobbie. And the others, too,

shouted: 'Take our love to Father!'

The old gentleman waved from his first-class carriage window. Quite violently he waved. And there was nothing odd in that, for he always had waved. But what was really remarkable was that from every window handkerchiefs fluttered, newspapers signalled, hands waved wildly. The train swept by with a rustle and roar, the little pebbles jumped and danced under it as it passed, and the children were left looking at each other.

'Well!' said Peter.

'*Well!*' said Bobbie.

'WELL!' said Phyllis.

'Whatever on earth does that mean?' asked Peter, but he did not expect any answer.

'I *don't* know,' said Bobbie. 'Perhaps the old gentleman told the people at his station to look out for us and wave. He knew we should like it!'

71

Now, curiously enough, this was just what had happened. The old gentleman, who was very well known and respected at this particular station, had got there early this morning, and he had waited at the door where the young man stands holding the interesting machine that clips the tickets, and he had said something to every single passenger who passed through that door. And after nodding to what the old gentleman had said – after the nods expressed every shade of surprise, interest, doubt, cheerful pleasure, and grumpy agreement – each passenger had gone on to the platform and read one certain part of his newspaper. And when the passengers got into the train, they had told the other passengers who were already there what the old gentleman had said, and then the other passengers had also looked at their newspapers and seemed very astonished and, mostly, pleased. Then, when the train passed the fence where the three children were, newspapers and hands and handkerchiefs were waved madly, till all that side of the train was fluttery with white, like pictures of the King's Coronation in the biography at Maskelyne and Cook's. To the children it almost seemed as though the train itself was alive, and was at last responding to the love that they had given it so freely and so long.

'It is most extraordinarily rum!' said Peter.

'Most stronery!' echoed Phyllis.

But Bobbie said, 'Don't you think the old gentleman's waves seemed more significating than usual?'

'No,' said the others.

'I do,' said Bobbie. 'I thought he was trying to explain something to us with his newspaper.'

'Explain what?' asked Peter, not unnaturally.

'*I* don't know,' Bobbie answered, 'but I do feel most awfully funny. I feel just exactly as if something was going to happen.'

'What is going to happen,' said Peter, 'is that Phyllis's stocking is going to come down.'

This was but too true. The suspender had given way in the agitation of the waves to the 9.15. Bobbie's handkerchief served as first aid to the injured, and they all went home.

Lessons were more than usually

difficult to Bobbie that day. Indeed, she disgraced herself so deeply over a quite simple sum about the division of 48 pounds of meat and 36 pounds of bread among 144 hungry children that Mother looked at her anxiously.

'Don't you feel quite well, dear?' she asked.

'I don't know,' was Bobbie's unexpected answer. 'I don't know how I feel. It isn't that I'm lazy. Mother, will you let me off lessons today? I feel as if I wanted to be quite alone by myself.'

'Yes, of course I'll let you off,' said Mother: 'but –'

Bobbie dropped her slate. It cracked just across the little green mark that is so useful for drawing patterns round, and it was never the same slate again. Without waiting to pick it up she bolted. Mother caught her in the hall feeling blindly among the waterproofs and umbrellas for her garden hat.

'What is it, my sweetheart?' said Mother. 'You don't feel ill, do you?'

'I *don't* know,' Bobbie answered, a little breathlessly, 'but I want to be by myself and see if my head really *is* all silly and my inside all squirmy-twisty.'

'Hadn't you better lie down?' Mother said, stroking her hair back from her forehead.

'I'd be more alive in the garden, I think,' said Bobbie.

But she could not stay in the garden. The hollyhocks and the asters and the late roses all seemed to be waiting for something to happen. It was one of those still, shiny autumn days, when everything does seem to be waiting.

Bobbie could not wait.

'I'll go down to the station,' she said, 'and talk to Perks and ask about the signalman's little boy.'

So she went down. On the way she passed the old lady from the Post-office, who gave her a kiss and a hug, but rather to Bobbie's surprise, no words except: 'God bless you, love –' and, after a pause, 'Run along – do.'

The draper's boy, who had sometimes been a little less than civil and a little more than contemptuous, now touched his cap, and uttered the remarkable words: ''Morning, Miss. I'm sure –'

The blacksmith, coming along with an open newspaper in his hand, was even more strange in his manner. He grinned broadly, though, as a rule, he was a man not given to smiles, and waved the newspaper long before he came up to her. And as he passed her, he said, in answer to her 'Good morning': 'Good morning to you, Missie, and many of them! I wish you joy, that I do!'

'Oh!' said Bobbie to herself, and her heart quickened its beats, 'something *is* going to happen! I know it is – everyone is so odd, like people are in dreams.'

The Station Master wrung her hand warmly. In fact he worked it up and down like a pump-handle. But he gave her no reason for this unusually enthusiastic greeting. He only said: 'The 11.54's a bit late, Miss – the extra luggage this holiday time,' and went away very quickly into that inner Temple of his into which even Bobbie dared not follow him.

Perks was not to be seen, and Bobbie shared the solitude of the platform with the Station Cat. This tortoise-shell lady, usually of a retiring disposition, came today to rub herself against the brown stockings of Bobbie with arched back, waving tail, and reverberating purrs.

'Dear me!' said Bobbie, stooping to stroke her, 'how very kind everybody is today – even you, pussy!'

Perks did not appear until the 11.54 was signalled, and then he, like everybody else that morning, had a newspaper in his hand.

'Hullo!' he said, ''ere you are. Well, if *this* is the train, it'll be smart work! Well, God bless you, my dear! I see it in the paper, and I don't think I was ever so glad of anything in all my born days!' He looked at Bobbie a moment, then said, 'One I must have, Miss, and no offence, I know, on a day like this 'ere!' and with that he kissed her, first on one cheek and then on the other.

'You ain't offended, are you?' he asked anxiously. 'I ain't took too great a liberty? On a day like this, you know –'

'No, no,' said Bobbie, 'of course it's not a liberty, dear Mr Perks; we love you quite as much as if you were an uncle of ours – but – on a day like *what*?'

'Like this 'ere!' said Perks. 'Don't I tell you I see it in the paper?'

'Saw *what* in the paper?' asked Bobbie, but already the 11.54 was steaming into the station and the Station Master was looking at all the places where Perks was not and ought to have been.

Bobbie was left standing alone, the Station Cat watching her from under the bench with friendly golden eyes.

Of course you know already exactly what was going to happen. Bobbie was not so clever. She had the vague, confused, expectant feeling that comes to one's heart in dreams. What her heart expected I can't tell – perhaps the very thing that you and I know was going to happen – but her mind expected nothing; it was almost blank, and felt nothing but tiredness and stupidity and an empty feeling like your body has when you have been a long walk and it is very far indeed past your proper dinnertime.

Only three people got out of the 11.54. The first was a countrywoman with two baskety boxes full of live chickens who stuck their russet heads out anxiously through the wicker bars; the second was Miss Peckitt, the grocer's wife's cousin, with a tin box and three brown-paper parcels; and the third –

'Oh! My Daddy, my Daddy!' That scream went like a knife into the heart of everyone in the train, and people put their heads out of the windows to see a tall pale man with lips set in a thin close line, and a little girl clinging to him with arms and legs, while his arms went tightly round her.

Lewis Carroll

ALICE IN WONDERLAND

ILLUSTRATED BY IAN BECK

THE QUEEN'S CROQUET-GROUND

*Alice has followed the White Rabbit down a rabbit-hole and finds herself
in Wonderland, where anything can happen.*

A LARGE rose-tree stood near the entrance of the garden:
the roses growing on it were white, but there were three
gardeners at it, busily painting them red. Alice thought this
a very curious thing, and she went nearer to watch them, and just as
she came up to them she heard one of them say, 'Look out now,
Five! Don't go splashing paint over me like that!'

'I couldn't help it,' said Five in a sulky tone. 'Seven jogged my
elbow.'

On which Seven looked up and said, 'That's right, Five! Always
lay the blame on others!'

'*You'd* better not talk!' said Five. 'I heard the Queen say only
yesterday you deserved to be beheaded!'

'What for?' said the one who had spoken first.

'That's none of *your* business, Two!' said Seven.

'Yes it *is* his business!' said Five, 'and I'll tell him — it was for bringing the cook tulip-roots instead of onions.'

Seven flung down his brush, and had just begun, 'Well, of all the unjust things —' when his eye chanced to fall upon Alice, as she stood watching them, and he checked himself suddenly: the others looked round also, and all of them bowed low.

'Would you tell me,' said Alice, a little timidly, 'why you are painting those roses?'

Five and Seven said nothing, but looked at Two. Two began in a low voice, 'Why the fact is, you see, Miss, this here ought to have been a *red* rose-tree, and we put a white one in by mistake; and if the Queen was to find out, we should all have our heads cut off, you know. So you see, Miss, we're doing our best afore she comes, to —' At this moment Five, who had been anxiously looking across the garden, called out, 'The Queen! The Queen!' and the three gardeners instantly threw themselves flat upon their faces. There was a sound of many footsteps, and Alice looked round, eager to see the Queen.

First came ten soldiers carrying clubs; these were all shaped like the three gardeners, oblong and flat, with their hands and feet at the corners: next the ten courtiers; these were ornamented all over with diamonds, and walked two and two, as the soldiers did. After these came the royal children; there were ten of them, and the little dears came jumping merrily along hand in hand, in couples; they were all ornamented with hearts. Next came the guests, mostly Kings and Queens, and among them Alice recognized the White Rabbit: it was talking in a hurried nervous manner, smiling at everything that was

said, and went by without noticing her. Then followed the Knave of Hearts, carrying the King's crown on a crimson velvet cushion; and, last of all this grand procession, came THE KING AND QUEEN OF HEARTS.

Alice was rather doubtful whether she ought not to lie down on her face like the three gardeners, but she could not remember ever having heard of such a rule at processions; 'and besides, what would be the use of a procession,' thought she, 'if people had all to lie down upon their faces, so that they couldn't see it?' So she stood still where she was, and waited.

When the procession came opposite to Alice, they all stopped and looked at her, and the Queen said severely, 'Who is this?' She said it to the Knave of Hearts, who only bowed and smiled in reply.

'Idiot!' said the Queen, tossing her head impatiently; and, turning to Alice, she went on, 'What's your name, child?'

'My name is Alice, so please Your Majesty,' said Alice very politely; but she added, to herself, 'Why, they're only a pack of cards, after all. I needn't be afraid of them!'

'And who are *these*?' said the Queen, pointing to the three gardeners who were lying round the rose-tree; for, you see, as they were lying on their faces, and the pattern on their backs was the same as the rest of the pack, she could not tell whether they were gardeners, or soldiers, or courtiers, or three of her own children.

'How should *I* know?' said Alice, surprised at her own courage. 'It's no business of *mine*.'

The Queen turned crimson with fury, and, after glaring at her for

a moment like a wild beast, screamed, 'Off with her head! Off –'

'Nonsense!' said Alice, very loudly and decidedly, and the Queen was silent.

The King laid his hand upon her arm, and timidly said, 'Consider, my dear: she is only a child!'

The Queen turned angrily away from him, and said to the Knave, 'Turn them over!'

The Knave did so, very carefully, with one foot.

'Get up!' said the Queen, in a shrill, loud voice, and the three gardeners instantly jumped up, and began bowing to the King, the Queen, the royal children, and everybody else.

'Leave off that!' screamed the Queen. 'You make me giddy.' And then, turning to the rose-tree, she went on, 'What *have* you been doing here?'

'May it please Your Majesty,' said Two, in a very humble tone, going down on one knee as he spoke, 'we were trying –'

'*I* see!' said the Queen, who had meanwhile been examining the roses. 'Off with their heads!' and the procession moved on, three of the soldiers remaining behind to execute the unfortunate gardeners, who ran to Alice for protection.

'You shan't be beheaded!' said Alice, and she put them into a large flower-pot that stood near. The three soldiers wandered about for a minute or two, looking for them, and then quietly marched off after the others.

'Are their heads off?' shouted the Queen.

'Their heads are gone, if it please Your Majesty!' the soldiers shouted in reply.

'That's right!' shouted the Queen. 'Can you play croquet?'

The soldiers were silent, and looked at Alice, as the question was evidently meant for her.

'Yes!' shouted Alice.

'Come on, then!' roared the Queen, and Alice joined the procession, wondering very much what would happen next.

'It's – it's a very fine day!' said a timid voice at her side. She was walking by the White Rabbit, who was peeping anxiously into her face.

'Very,' said Alice: '– where's the Duchess?'

'Hush! Hush!' said the Rabbit in a low, hurried tone. He looked anxiously over his shoulder as he spoke, and then raised himself upon tiptoe, put his mouth close to her ear, and whispered, 'She's under sentence of execution.'

'What for?' said Alice.

'Did you say "What a pity!"?' the Rabbit asked.

'No, I didn't,' said Alice. 'I don't think it's at all a pity. I said, "What for?"'

'She boxed the Queen's ears –' the Rabbit began. Alice gave a little scream of laughter. 'Oh, hush!' the Rabbit whispered in a frightened tone. 'The Queen will hear you! You see, she came rather late, and the Queen said –'

'Get to your places!' shouted the Queen in a voice of thunder, and people began running about in all directions, tumbling up against each other; however, they got settled down in a minute or two, and the game began. Alice thought she had never seen such a curious croquet-ground in all her life; it was all ridges and furrows; the balls were live hedgehogs, the mallets live flamingoes, and the soldiers had to double themselves up and stand on their hands and feet, to make the arches.

The chief difficulty Alice found at first was in managing her flamingo: she succeeded in getting its body tucked away, comfortably enough, under her arm, with its legs hanging down, but generally, just as she had got its neck nicely straightened out, and was going to give the hedgehog a blow with its head, it *would* twist itself round and look up in her face, with such a puzzled expression that she could not help bursting out laughing: and when she had got its head down, and was going to begin again, it was very provoking to find that the hedgehog had unrolled itself, and was in the act of crawling away: besides all this, there was generally a ridge or furrow in the way wherever she wanted to send the hedgehog to, and, as the doubled-up soldiers were always getting up and walking off to other parts of the ground, Alice soon came to the conclusion that it was a very difficult game indeed.

The players all played at once without waiting for turns, quarrelling all the while, and fighting for the hedgehogs; and in a very short time the Queen was in a furious passion, and went stamping about, and shouting, 'Off with his head!' or, 'Off with her head!' about once a minute.

∾

Susan Coolidge

WHAT KATY DID

ILLUSTRATED BY SHIRLEY HUGHES

THE DAY OF SCRAPES

Lively, quick-tempered Katy always means to be well-behaved, but somehow all her good intentions get forgotten or go horribly wrong!

MRS Knight's school, to which Katy and Clover and Cecy went, stood quite at the other end of the town from Dr Carr's. It was a low, one-storey building, and had a yard behind it, in which the girls played at recess. Unfortunately, next door to it was Miss Miller's school, equally large and popular, and with a yard behind it also. Only a high board fence separated the two playgrounds.

Mrs Knight was a stout, gentle woman, who moved slowly, and had a face which made you think of an amiable and well-disposed cow. Miss Miller, on the contrary, had black eyes, with black corkscrew curls waving about them, and was generally brisk and snappy. A constant feud raged between the two schools as to the respective merits of the teachers and the instruction. The Knight girls, for some unknown reason, considered themselves genteel and the Miller girls vulgar, and took no pains to conceal this opinion; while the Miller girls, on the other hand, retaliated by being as aggravating as they knew how. They spent their recesses and intermissions mostly in making faces through the knot-holes in the fence, and over the top of it, when they could get there, which wasn't an easy thing to do, as the fence was pretty high. The Knight girls could make faces too, for all their gentility. Their yard had one great advantage over the other: it possessed a wood-shed, with a climbable roof, which commanded Miss Miller's premises, and upon this the girls used to sit in rows, turning up their noses at the next yard, and irritating the foe by jeering remarks. 'Knights' and 'Millerites' the two schools called each other; and the feud raged so high that sometimes it was hardly safe for a Knight to meet a Millerite in the street; all of which, as may be imagined, was exceedingly improving both to the manners and morals of the young ladies concerned.

One morning, not long after the day in Paradise, Katy was late. She could not find her things. Her algebra, as she expressed it, had 'gone and lost itself', her slate was missing, and the string was off her sun-bonnet. She ran about, searching for these articles and banging doors, till Aunt Izzie was out of patience.

'As for your algebra,' she said, 'if it is that very dirty book with only one cover, and scribbled all over the leaves, you will find it under the kitchen table. Philly was playing before breakfast that it was a pig; no wonder, I'm sure, for it looks good for nothing else. How you do manage to spoil your school-books in this manner, Katy, I cannot imagine. It is less than a month since your father got you a new algebra, and look at it now – not fit to be carried about. I do wish you'd realize what books cost!

'About your slate,' she went on, 'I know nothing; but here is the bonnet-string;' taking it out of her pocket.

'Oh, thank you!' said Katy, hastily sticking it on with a pin.

'Katy Carr!' almost screamed Miss Izzie, 'what *are* you about? Pinning on your bonnet string! Mercy on me! What shiftless thing will you do next? Now stand still and don't fidget! You shan't stir till I have sewed it on properly.'

It wasn't easy to 'stand still and not fidget', with Aunt Izzie fussing away and lecturing, and now and then, in a moment of forgetfulness, sticking her needle into one's chin. Katy bore it as well as she could, only shifting perpetually from one foot to the other, and now and then uttering a little snort, like an impatient horse. The minute she was released she flew into the kitchen, seized the algebra, and rushed like a whirlwind to the gate, where good little Clover stood patiently waiting, though all ready herself, and terribly afraid she should be late.

'We shall have to run,' gasped Katy, quite out of breath. 'Aunt Izzie kept me. She has been so horrid!'

They did run as fast as they could, but time ran faster. And before they were half-way to school the town clock struck nine, and all the hope was over. This vexed Katy very much; for, though often late, she was always eager to be early.

'There,' she said, stopping short, 'I shall just tell Aunt Izzie that it was her fault. It is *too* bad.' And she marched into school in a very cross mood.

A day begun in this manner is pretty sure to end badly, as most of us know. All the morning through things seemed to go wrong. Katy missed twice in her grammar lesson, and lost her place in the class. Her hand shook so when she copied her composition, that the writing, not good at best, turned out almost illegible, so that Mrs Knight said it must be all done over again. This made Katy crosser than ever; and almost before she thought, she had whispered to Clover, 'How hateful!' And then, when just before recess all who had been speaking were requested to stand up, her conscience gave such

a twinge that she was forced to get up with the rest, and see a black mark put against her name on the list. The tears came into her eyes from vexation; and, for fear the other girls would notice them, she made a bolt for the yard as soon as the bell rang, and mounted up all alone to the wood-house roof, where she sat with her back to the school, fighting with her eyes, and trying to get her face in order before the rest should come.

Miss Miller's clock was about four minutes slower than Mrs Knight's, so the next playground was empty. It was a warm, breezy day, and as Katy sat there, suddenly a gust of wind came, and seizing her sun-bonnet, which was only half tied on, whirled it across the roof. She clutched after it as it flew, but too late. Once, twice, thrice it flapped, then it disappeared over the edge, and Katy, flying after, saw it lying in a crumpled lilac heap in the very middle of the enemy's yard.

This was horrible! Not merely losing the bonnet, for Katy was comfortably indifferent as to what became of her clothes, but to lose it so. In another minute the Miller girls would be out. Already she seemed to see them dancing war-dances round the unfortunate bonnet, pinning it on a pole, using it as a football, waving it over the fence, and otherwise treating it as Indians treat a captive taken in war. Was it to be endured? Never! Better die first! And with very much the feeling of a person who faces destruction rather than forfeit honour, Katy set her teeth, and, sliding rapidly down the roof, seized the fence, and with one bold leap vaulted into Miss Miller's yard.

Just then the recess bell tinkled; and a little Millerite who sat by the window, and who, for two seconds, had been dying to give the exciting information, squeaked out to the others: 'There's Katy Carr in our backyard!'

Out poured the Millerites, big and little. Their wrath and indignation at this daring invasion cannot be described. With a howl of fury they precipitated themselves upon Katy, but she was as quick as they, and holding the rescued bonnet in her hand, was already halfway up the fence.

There are moments when it is a fine thing to be tall. On this occasion Katy's long legs and arms served her an excellent turn. Nothing but a Daddy Longlegs ever climbed so fast or so wildly as she did now. In one second she had gained the top of the fence. Just as she went over a Millerite seized her by the last foot, and almost dragged her boot off.

Almost, not quite, thanks to the stout thread with which Aunt Izzie had sewed on the buttons. With a frantic kick Katy released herself, and had the satisfaction of seeing her assailant go head over heels backwards, while, with a shriek of triumph and fright, she herself plunged headlong into the midst of a group of Knights. They were listening with open mouths to the uproar, and now stood transfixed at the astonishing spectacle of one of their number absolutely returning alive from the camp of the enemy.

I cannot tell you what a commotion ensued. The Knights were beside themselves with pride and triumph. Katy was kissed and hugged, and made to tell her story over and over again, while rows of exulting girls sat on the wood-house roof to crow over the discomfited Millerites: and when, later, the foe rallied and began to retort over the fence, Clover, armed with a tack hammer, was lifted up in the arms of one of the tall girls to rap the intruding knuckles

as they appeared on the top. This she did with such goodwill that
the Millerites were glad to drop down again, and mutter vengeance
at a safe distance. Altogether it was a great day for the school, a day
to be remembered. As time went on, Katy, what with the excitement
of her adventure and of being praised and petted by the big girls,
grew perfectly reckless, and hardly knew what she said or did.

Johanna Spyri

HEIDI

ILLUSTRATED BY DAVID FRANKLAND

HEIDI ARRIVES AT HER
GRANDFATHER'S HUT

As soon as Detie had disappeared, the old man sat down again on the bench. He stared at the ground in silence, blowing great clouds of smoke from his pipe, while Heidi explored her new surroundings with delight. She went up to the goat stall which was built on to the side of the hut, but found it empty. Then she went round to the back and stood for a while listening to the noise the wind made whistling through the branches of the old fir trees. Presently it died down, and she came back to the front of the hut, where she found her grandfather still sitting in the same position. As she stood watching him, hands behind her back, he looked up and said, 'What do you want to do now?'

'I want to see what is inside the hut,' she answered.

'Come on, then,' he said, and he got up and led the way indoors. 'Bring the bundle of clothes in with you,' he added.

'I shan't want them any more,' she declared.

The old man turned and looked sharply at her, and saw her black eyes shining with anticipation.

'She's no fool,' he muttered to himself, and added aloud, 'Why's that?'

'I want to be able to run about like the goats do.'

'Well, so you can,' said her grandfather, 'but bring the things inside all the same. They can go in the cupboard.'

Heidi picked up the bundle and followed the old man into a biggish room which was the whole extent of his living quarters. She saw a table and a chair, and his bed over in one corner. Opposite that was a stove, over which a big pot was hanging. There was a door in one wall which the old man opened, and she saw it was a large cupboard with his clothes hanging in it. There were shelves in it too. One held his shirts, socks, and handkerchiefs, another plates, cups, and glasses, while on the top one were a round loaf, some smoked meat, and some cheese. Here, in fact, were all the old man's possessions. Heidi went inside the open cupboard and pushed her bundle right away to the back so that it would not easily be seen again.

'Where shall I sleep, Grandfather?' she asked next.

'Where you like,' he replied.

This answer pleased Heidi, and as she was looking round the room for a good place she noticed a ladder propped against the wall near her grandfather's bed. She climbed up it at once and found herself in a hay loft. A pile of fresh, sweet-smelling hay lay there, and there was a round hole in the wall of the loft, through which she could see right down the valley.

'I shall sleep up here,' she called down. 'It's a splendid place. Just come and see, Grandfather.'

'I know it well,' he called back.

'I'm going to make my bed now,' she went on, 'but you'll have to come up and bring me a sheet to lie on.'

'All right,' said her grandfather, and he went to the cupboard and searched among his belongings until he found a piece of coarse cloth, which he carried up to her. He found she had already made herself a sort of mattress and pillow of the hay, and had placed them so that she would be able to look through the hole in the wall when she was in bed.

'That's right,' said the old man, 'but it needs to be thicker than that,' and he spread a lot more hay over hers so that she would not feel the hard floor through it. The thick cloth which he had brought for a sheet was so heavy that she could hardly lift it by herself, but its thickness made it a good protection against the prickly hay stalks. Together they spread it out, and Heidi tucked the ends under her 'mattress' to make it all neat and comfortable. Then she looked at her bed thoughtfully for a moment, and said, 'We've forgotten something, Grandfather.'

'What's that?' he asked.

'A blanket to cover it, so that I can creep under it when I go to bed.'

'That's what you think, is it? Suppose I haven't got one?'

'Oh, well then, it doesn't matter,' said Heidi, 'I can easily cover myself with hay,' and she was just going to fetch some more when her grandfather stopped her. 'Wait a bit,' he said, and he went down the ladder, and took from his own bed a great sack made of heavy linen which he brought up to the loft.

'There, isn't that better than hay?' he asked, as they put it over the bed. Heidi was delighted with the result.

'That's a wonderful blanket, and my whole bed's lovely. I wish it was bedtime now so that I could get in it.'

'I think we might have something to eat first, don't you?' said her grandfather. Heidi had forgotten everything else in her excitement over the bed, but at the mention of food, she realized how hungry she was, as she had eaten nothing all day except a piece of bread and a cup of weak coffee before setting out on her long journey. So she replied eagerly, 'Oh, yes.'

'Well then, if we are agreed, let us go and see about a meal,' and he followed Heidi down the ladder. He went to the stove, lifted the big pot off the chain and put a smaller one in its place, then sat himself down on a three-legged stool and blew up the fire with the bellows till it was red and glowing. As the pot began to sing, he put a large piece of cheese on a toasting fork and moved it to and fro in front of the fire until it became golden yellow all over. At first Heidi just stood and watched with great interest, then she thought of something else and ran to the cupboard. When her grandfather brought the steaming pot and the toasted cheese to the table, he found it was laid with two plates, two knives, and the round loaf. Heidi had noticed these things in the cupboard and knew they would be needed for the meal.

'I'm glad to see you can think things out for yourself,' he said, 'but there is something missing.'

Heidi looked at the steaming pot and went back to the cupboard. She could see one mug there and two glasses, so she took the mug and one of the glasses and put them on the table.

'That's right. You know how to be helpful,' said her grandfather. 'Now where are you going to sit?' He himself was in the only chair so Heidi fetched the three-legged stool and sat down on that.

'You've got a seat all right, but rather a low one, and even with my chair you would not be high enough to reach the table.' So saying, the old man got up and pushed his chair in front of Heidi's stool and put the mug filled with milk on it, and a plate on which was a slice of bread covered with the golden toasted cheese. 'Now you have a table to yourself and can start to eat,' he said . . .

After the meal her grandfather went to the goat-stall and Heidi watched him sweep the floor with a broom and then put down fresh straw for the animals to sleep on. When that job was done he went into the shed, which was built on to the side of the hut, and sawed off several round sticks of wood. Then he bored holes to fit them in a strong flat piece of board, and when he had fitted them all together, the result was a high chair. Heidi watched him, silent in her amazement.

'Do you know what this is?' he asked, when he had finished.

'It's a chair specially for me,' she said wonderingly. 'And how quickly you made it!'

'She's got eyes in her head and knows how to use them,' thought the old man. Next he busied himself with some small repairs in the hut, driving in a nail here and there, tightening a screw in the door and so on. Heidi followed at his heels, watching him with the closest attention, for everything was new and interesting to her . . .

Suddenly there was a shrill whistle and Peter appeared in the midst of his herd of goats. Heidi gave a cry of delight and rushed to greet her friends of the morning. As the goats reached the hut they all stood still, except for two graceful animals, one brown and one white, which detached themselves from the others and went up to the old man. Then they began to lick his hands for he was holding a little salt in them, as he did every evening to welcome them home.

Peter went away with the rest of the herd, and Heidi ran to the two goats and began to pat them gently. 'Are these ours, Grandfather?' she asked. 'Both of them? Do they go into the stall? Will they always be here with us?' Her questions followed so closely on each other that her grandfather could hardly get an answer in edgeways. When the goats had finished the salt, the old man said, 'Now go and fetch your mug and the bread.' She obeyed and was back in a flash. Then he filled her mug with milk from the white goat and gave it to her with a slice of bread. 'Eat that and then go to bed,' he said. 'If you want a nightdress or anything like that, you'll find it in the bundle your aunt brought. Now I must see to the goats. Sleep well.'

'Good night, Grandfather,' she called, as he walked off with

the animals. Then she ran after them to ask what the goats'
names were.

'The white one is called Daisy and the brown Dusky,' replied
her grandfather.

'Good night, Daisy, good night, Dusky,' called Heidi after the
goats, who had disappeared into their stall. She ate her supper
on the bench outside the hut. The wind was so strong, it almost
blew her away, so she finished her bread and milk quickly and
went indoors and up to bed. There she was soon sleeping as
soundly as if she was tucked up in the finest bed in the world.

Mrs Molesworth

THE CUCKOO CLOCK

ILLUSTRATED BY JUSTIN TODD

BUTTERFLY-LAND

Griselda is staying with her two sweet but rather dull old aunts.
At first she is very bored, but then she discovers that the cuckoo clock is
magic and the cuckoo can take her to the most wonderful places.

GRISELDA opened her eyes.

What did she see?

The loveliest, loveliest garden that ever or never a little girl's eyes saw. As for describing it, I cannot. I must leave a good deal to your fancy. It was just a *delicious* garden. There was a charming mixture of all that is needed. to make a garden perfect – grass, velvety lawn rather; water, for a little brook ran tinkling in and out, playing bo-peep among the bushes; trees, of course, and flowers, of course, flowers of every shade and shape. But all these beautiful things Griselda did not at first give as much attention to as they deserved; her eyes were so occupied with a quite unusual sight that met them.

This was butterflies! Not that butterflies are so very uncommon, but butterflies, as Griselda saw them, I am quite sure, children, none of you ever saw, or are likely to see. There were such enormous numbers of them, and the variety of their colours and sizes was so great. They were fluttering about everywhere; the garden seemed actually alive with them.

Griselda stood for a moment in silent delight, feasting her eyes on the lovely things before her, enjoying the delicious sunshine which kissed her poor little bare feet, and seemed to wrap her all up in its warm embrace. Then she turned to her little friend.

'Cuckoo,' she said, 'I thank you *so* much. This is fairyland, at last!'

The cuckoo smiled, I was going to say, but that would be a figure of speech only, would it not? He shook his head gently.

'No, Griselda,' he said kindly; 'this is only butterfly-land.'

'*Butterfly*-land!' repeated Griselda, with a little disappointment in her tone.

'Well,' said the cuckoo, 'it's where you were wishing to be yesterday, isn't it?'

Griselda did not particularly like these allusions to 'yesterday'. She thought it would be as well to change the subject.

'It's a beautiful place, whatever it is,' she said, 'and I'm sure, cuckoo, I'm *very* much obliged to you for bringing me here. Now may I run about and look at everything? How delicious it is to feel the warm sunshine again! I didn't know how cold I was. Look, cuckoo, my toes and fingers are quite blue; they're only just beginning to come right again. I suppose the sun always shines here. How nice it must be to be a butterfly; don't you think so, cuckoo? Nothing to do but fly about.'

She stopped at last, quite out of breath.

'Griselda,' said the cuckoo, 'if you want me to answer your questions, you must ask them one at a time. You may run about and look at everything if you like, but you had better not be in such a hurry. You will make a great many mistakes if you are – you have made some already.'

'How?' said Griselda.

'*Have* the butterflies nothing to do but fly about? Watch them.'
Griselda watched.

'They do seem to be doing something,' she said, at last, 'but I can't think what. They seem to be nibbling at the flowers, and then flying away, something like bees gathering honey. *Butterflies* don't gather honey, cuckoo?'

'No,' said the cuckoo. 'They are filling their paintboxes.'

'What *do* you mean?' said Griselda.

'Come and see,' said the cuckoo.

He flew quietly along in front of her, leading the way through the prettiest paths in all the pretty garden. The paths were arranged in different colours, as it were; that is to say, the flowers growing along their sides were not all 'mixty-maxty', but one shade after another in regular order – from the palest blush pink to the very deepest damask crimson; then, again, from the soft greenish blue of the small grass forget-me-not to the rich warm tinge of the brilliant cornflower. *Every* tint was there; shades, to which, though not exactly strange to her, Griselda could yet have given no name, for the daisy dew, you see, had sharpened her eyes to observe delicate variations of colour, as she had never done before.

'How beautifully the flowers are planned,' she said to the cuckoo. 'Is it just to look pretty, or why?'

'It saves time,' replied the cuckoo. 'The fetch-and-carry butterflies know exactly where to go to for the tint the world-flower-painters want.'

'Who are the fetch-and-carry butterflies, and who are the world-flower-painters?' asked Griselda.

'Wait a bit and you'll see, and use your eyes,' answered the cuckoo. 'It'll do your tongue no harm to have a rest now and then.'

Griselda thought it as well to take his advice, though not particularly relishing the manner in which it was given. She did use her eyes, and as she and the cuckoo made their way along the flower alleys, she saw that the butterflies were never idle. They came regularly, in little parties of twos and threes, and nibbled away, as she called it, at flowers of the same colour but different shades, till they had got what they wanted. Then off flew butterfly No. 1 with perhaps the palest tint of maize, of yellow, or lavender, whichever he was in quest of, followed by No. 2 with the next deeper shade of the

same, and No. 3 bringing up the rear.

Griselda gave a little sigh.

'What's the matter?' said the cuckoo.

'They work very hard,' she replied, in a melancholy tone.

'It's a busy time of year,' observed the cuckoo, drily.

After a while they came to what seemed to be a sort of centre to the garden. It was a huge glasshouse, with numberless doors, in and out of which butterflies were incessantly flying – reminding Griselda again of bees and a beehive. But she made no remark till the cuckoo spoke again.

'Come in,' he said.

Griselda had to stoop a good deal, but she did manage to get in without knocking her head or doing any damage. Inside was just a mass of butterflies. A confused mass it seemed at first, but after a while she saw that it was the very reverse of confused. The butterflies were all settled in rows on long, narrow, white tables, and before each was a tiny object about the size of a flattened-out pin's head, which he was most carefully painting with one of his tentacles, which, from time to time, he moistened by rubbing it on the head of a butterfly waiting patiently behind him. Behind this butterfly again stood another, who after a while took his place, while the first attendant flew away.

'To fill his paintbox again,' remarked the cuckoo, who seemed to read Griselda's thoughts.

'But what *are* they painting, cuckoo?' she inquired eagerly.

'All the flowers in the world,' replied the cuckoo. 'Autumn, winter, and spring, they're hard at work. It's only just for the three months of summer that the butterflies have any holiday, and then a few stray ones now and then wander up to the world, and people talk about "idle butterflies"! And even then it isn't true that they are idle. They go up to take a look at the flowers, to see how their work has turned out, and many a damaged petal they repair, or touch up a faded tint, though no one ever knows it.'

'*I* know it now,' said Griselda. 'I will never talk about idle butterflies again – never. But, cuckoo, do they paint all the flowers *here*, too? What a *fearful* lot they must have to do!'

'No,' said the cuckoo, 'the flowers down here are fairy flowers. They never fade or die, they are always just as you see them. But the colours of your flowers are all taken from them, as you have seen. Of course they don't look the same up there,' he went on, with a slight contemptuous shrug of his cuckoo shoulders. 'The coarse air and the ugly things about must take the bloom off. The wild flowers do

the best, to my thinking; people don't meddle with them in their stupid, clumsy way.'

'But how do they get the flowers sent up to the world, cuckoo?' asked Griselda.

'They're packed up, of course, and taken up at night when all of you are asleep,' said the cuckoo. 'They're painted on elastic stuff, you see, which fits itself as the plant grows. Why, if your eyes were as they are usually, Griselda, you couldn't even *see* the petals the butterflies are painting now.'

'And the packing up,' said Griselda, 'do the butterflies do that too?'

'No,' said the cuckoo, 'the fairies look after that.'

'How wonderful!' exclaimed Griselda. But before the cuckoo had time to say more a sudden tumult filled the air. It was butterfly dinner-time!

∾

Anna Sewell

BLACK BEAUTY

ILLUSTRATED BY RICHARD JONES

POOR GINGER

Black Beauty tells the story of his life over a hundred years ago in Victorian England. Some of Beauty's memories are happy, some are sad, but few are as moving as when he meets his old friend Ginger.

ONE day, whilst our cab and many others were waiting outside one of the Parks, where a band was playing, a shabby old cab drove up beside ours. The horse was an old worn-out chestnut, with an ill-kept coat, and bones that showed plainly through it. The knees knuckled over, and the forelegs were very unsteady. I had been eating some hay, and the wind rolled a little lock of it that way, and the poor creature put out her long thin neck and picked it up, and then turned round and looked about for more. There was a hopeless look in the dull eye that I could not help noticing, and then, as I was thinking where I had seen that horse before, she looked full at me and said, 'Black Beauty, is that you?'

It was Ginger! But how changed! The beautifully arched and

glossy neck was now straight and lank, and fallen in, the clean straight legs and delicate fetlocks were swelled; the joints were grown out of shape with hard work; the face, that was once so full of spirit and life, was now full of suffering, and I could tell by the heaving of her sides, and her frequent cough, how bad her breath was.

Our drivers were standing together a little way off, so I sidled up to her a step or two, that we might have a little quiet talk. It was a sad tale that she had to tell.

After a twelvemonth's run off at Earlshall, she was considered to be fit for work again, and was sold to a gentleman. For a little while she got on very well, but after a longer gallop than usual the old strain returned, and after being rested and doctored she was again sold. In this way she changed hands several times, but always getting lower down.

'And so at last,' said she, 'I was bought by a man who keeps a number of cabs and horses, and lets them out. You look well off, and I am glad of it, but I could not tell you what my life has been. When they found out my weakness, they said I was not worth what they gave for me, and that I must go into one of the low cabs, and just be used up; that is what they are doing, whipping and working me with never one thought of what I suffer; they paid for me, and must get it out of me, they say. The man who hires me now pays a deal of money to the owner every day, and so he has to get it out of me too; and so it's all the week round and round, with never a Sunday rest.'

I said, 'You used to stand up for yourself if you were ill-used.'

'Ah!' she said, 'I did once, but it's no use; men are strongest, and if they are cruel and have no feeling, there is nothing that we can do, but just bear it, bear it on and on to the end. I wish the end was come, I wish I was dead. I have seen dead horses, and I am sure they do not suffer pain. I wish I may drop down dead at my work, and not be sent off to the knacker's.'

I was very much troubled, and I put my nose up to hers, but I could say nothing to comfort her. I think she was pleased to see me, for she said, 'You are the only friend I ever had.'

Just then her driver came up, and with a tug at her mouth backed her out of the line and drove off, leaving me very sad indeed.

A short time after this a cart with a dead horse in it passed our cab-stand. The head hung out of the cart-tail, the lifeless tongue was slowly dropping with blood; and the sight was too dreadful. It was a chestnut horse with a long thin neck. I saw a white streak down the forehead. I believe it was Ginger; I hoped it was, for then her troubles would be over. Oh! If men were more merciful, they would shoot us before we came to such misery.

∽

Kenneth Grahame

THE WIND
IN THE WILLOWS

ILLUSTRATED BY MIKE TERRY

THE FURTHER
ADVENTURES OF TOAD

*Toad has escaped from prison disguised as a washerwoman. Now he is
on his way back to Toad Hall, feeling very pleased with himself.*

TOAD got so puffed up with conceit that he made up a
song as he walked in praise of himself, and sang it at the
top of his voice, though there was no one to hear it but
him. It was perhaps the most conceited song that any animal ever
composed:

> The world has held great Heroes,
> As history-books have showed;
> But never a name to go down to fame
> Compared with that of Toad!

The clever men at Oxford
   Know all that there is to be knowed.
But they none of them know one half as much
   As intelligent Mr Toad!

The animals sat in the Ark and cried,
   Their tears in torrents flowed.
Who was it said, 'There's land ahead'?
   Encouraging Mr Toad!

The Army all saluted
   As they marched along the road.
Was it the King? Or Kitchener?
   No. It was Mr Toad.

The Queen and her Ladies-in-waiting
   Sat at the window and sewed.
She cried, 'Look! who's that *handsome* man?'
   They answered, 'Mr Toad.'

There was a great deal more of the same sort, but too dreadfully conceited to be written down. These are some of the milder verses.

He sang as he walked, and he walked as he sang, and got more inflated every minute. But his pride was shortly to have a severe fall.

After some miles of country lanes he reached the high road, and as he turned into it and glanced along its white length, he saw approaching him a speck that turned into a dot and then into a blob,

and then into something very familiar; and a double note of warning, only too well known, fell on his delighted ear.

'This is something like!' said the excited Toad. 'This is real life again, this is once more the great world from which I have been missed so long! I will hail them, my brothers of the wheel, and pitch them a yarn, of the sort that has been so successful hitherto; and they will give me a lift, of course, and then I will talk to them some more; and perhaps, with luck, it may even end in my driving up to Toad Hall in a motor-car! That will be one in the eye for Badger!'

He stepped confidently out into the road to hail the motor-car, which came along at an easy pace, slowing down as it neared the lane; when suddenly he became very pale, his heart turned to water, his knees shook and yielded under him, and he doubled up and collapsed with a sickening pain in his interior. And well he might, the unhappy animal; for the approaching car was the very one he had stolen out of the yard of the Red Lion Hotel on that fatal day when all his troubles began! And the people in it were the very same people he had sat and watched at luncheon in the coffee-room!

He sank down in a shabby, miserable heap in the road, murmuring to himself in his despair, 'It's all up! · It's all over now! Chains and policemen again! Prison again! Dry bread and water again! O, what a fool I have been! What did I want to go strutting about the country for, singing conceited songs, and hailing people in broad day on the high road, instead of hiding till nightfall and slipping home quietly by back ways! O hapless Toad! O ill-fated animal!'

The terrible motor-car drew slowly nearer and nearer, till at last he heard it stop just short of him. Two gentlemen got out and walked round the trembling heap of crumpled misery lying in the road, and one of them said, 'O dear! This is very sad! Here is a poor old thing – a washerwoman apparently – who has fainted in the road! Perhaps she is overcome by the heat, poor creature; or possibly she has not had any food today. Let us lift her into the car and take her to the nearest village, where doubtless she has friends.'

They tenderly lifted Toad into the motor-car and propped him up with soft cushions, and proceeded on their way.

When Toad heard them talk in so kind and sympathetic a manner, he knew that he was not recognized, his courage began to revive, and he cautiously opened first one eye and then the other.

'Look!' said one of the gentlemen, 'she is better already. The fresh air is doing her good. How do you feel now, ma'am?'

'Thank you kindly, sir,' said Toad in a feeble voice, 'I'm feeling a great deal better!'

'That's right,' said the gentleman. 'Now keep quite still, and, above all, don't try to talk.'

'I won't,' said Toad. 'I was only thinking, if I might sit on the front seat there, beside the driver, where I could get the fresh air full in my face, I should soon be all right again.'

'What a very sensible woman!' said the gentleman. 'Of course you shall.' So they carefully helped Toad into the front seat beside the driver, and on they went once more.

Toad was almost himself again by now. He sat up, looked about him, and tried to beat down the tremors, the yearnings, the old cravings that rose up and beset him and took possession of him entirely.

'It is fate!' he said to himself. 'Why strive? Why struggle?' and he turned to the driver at his side.

'Please, sir,' he said, 'I wish you would kindly let me try and drive the car for a little. I've been watching you carefully, and it looks so easy and so interesting, and I should like to be able to tell my friends that once I had driven a motor-car!'

The driver laughed at the proposal, so heartily that the gentleman inquired what the matter was. When he heard, he said, to Toad's delight, 'Bravo, ma'am! I like your spirit. Let her have a try, and look after her. She won't do any harm.'

Toad eagerly scrambled into the seat vacated by the driver, took the steering-wheel in his hands, listened with affected

humility to the instructions given him, and set the car in motion, but very slowly and carefully at first, for he was determined to be prudent.

The gentlemen behind clapped their hands and applauded, and Toad heard them saying, 'How well she does it! Fancy a washerwoman driving a car as well as that, the first time!'

Toad went a little faster;

then faster still, and faster.

He heard the gentlemen call out warningly, 'Be careful, washerwoman!' And this annoyed him, and he began to lose his head.

The driver tried to interfere, but he pinned him down in his seat with one elbow, and put on full speed. The rush of air in his face, the hum of the engine, and the light jump of the car beneath him intoxicated his weak brain. 'Washerwoman, indeed!' he shouted recklessly. 'Ho, ho! I am the Toad, the motor-car snatcher, the prison-breaker, the Toad who always escapes! Sit still, and you shall know what driving really is, for you are in the hands of the famous, the skilful, the entirely fearless Toad!'

With a cry of horror the whole party rose and flung themselves on him. 'Seize him!' they cried. 'Seize the Toad, the wicked animal who stole our motor-car! Bind him, chain him, drag him to the nearest police-station! Down with the desperate and dangerous Toad!'

Alas! They should have thought, they ought to have been more prudent, they should have remembered to stop the motor-car somehow before playing any pranks of that sort. With a half-turn of the wheel the Toad sent the car crashing through the low hedge that ran along the roadside. One mighty bound, a violent shock, and the wheels of the car were churning up the thick mud of a horse-pond.

Toad found himself flying through the air with the strong upward rush and delicate curve of a swallow. He liked the motion, and was just beginning to wonder whether it would go on until he developed wings and turned into a Toad-bird, when he landed on his back with a thump, in the soft rich grass of a meadow. Sitting up, he could just see the motor-car in the pond, nearly submerged; the gentlemen and the driver, encumbered by their long coats, were floundering helplessly in the water.

He picked himself up rapidly and set off running across country as hard as he could, scrambling through hedges, jumping ditches, pounding across fields till he was breathless and weary, and had to settle down into an easy walk. When he had recovered his breath somewhat, and was able to think calmly, he began to giggle, and from giggling he took to laughing, and he laughed till he had to sit down under a hedge. 'Ho, ho!' he cried, in ecstasies of self-admiration. 'Toad again! Toad, as usual, comes out on the top! Who was it got them to give him a lift? Who managed to get

on the front seat for the sake of fresh air? Who persuaded them into letting him see if he could drive? Who landed them all in a horse-pond? Who escaped, flying gaily and unscathed through the air, leaving the narrow-minded, grudging, timid excursionists in the mud where they should rightly be? Why, Toad, of course; clever Toad, great Toad, *good* Toad!'

Then he burst into song again, and chanted with uplifted voice:

> The motor-car went Poop-poop-poop,
>   As it raced along the road.
> Who was it steered it into a pond?
>   Ingenious Mr Toad!

'Oh, how clever I am! How clever, how clever, how very clev–'

A slight noise at a distance behind him made him turn his head and look. O horror! O misery! O despair!

About two fields off, a chauffeur in his leather gaiters and two large rural policemen were visible, running towards him as hard as they could go!

Poor Toad sprang to his feet and pelted away again, his heart in his mouth. 'O my!' he gasped, as he panted along, 'what an *ass* I am! What a *conceited* and heedless ass! Swaggering again! Shouting and singing songs again! Sitting still and gassing again! O my! O my! O my!'

He glanced back, and saw to his dismay that they were gaining on him. On he ran desperately, but kept looking back, and saw that they still gained steadily. He did his best, but he was a fat animal, and his legs were short, and still they gained. He could hear them close behind him now. Ceasing to heed where he was going, he struggled on blindly and wildly, looking back over his shoulder at the now triumphant enemy, when suddenly the earth failed under his feet, he grasped at the air, and, splash! he found himself head over ears in deep water, rapid water, water that bore him along with a force he could not contend with; and he knew that in his blind panic he had run straight into the river!

INDEX OF AUTHORS

ACKNOWLEDGEMENTS

~

*The editor and publishers gratefully acknowledge the following
for permission to reproduce copyright stories in this book:*

'Humblepuppy' by Joan Aiken from *A Harp of Fishbones*, published by Jonathan Cape, copyright © Joan Aiken Enterprises Ltd, 1972 UK, copyright © Joan Aiken, 1971 US, reprinted by permission of A. M. Heath & Company Limited; 'The Emperor's New Clothes' retold by Wendy Cooling, copyright © Wendy Cooling, 1996, reprinted by kind permission of the author; 'The Further Adventures of Toad' by Kenneth Grahame from *The Wind in the Willows*, published by Methuen 1908, copyright © The University Chest, 1908, reprinted by permission of Curtis Brown Ltd, London; 'How the Camel Got His Hump' by Rudyard Kipling from *Just So Stories*, published by Macmillan 1902, copyright © The National Trust for Places of Historic Interest and Natural Beauty, 1902, reprinted by permission of A. P. Watt Ltd on behalf of The National Trust for Places of Historic Interest and Natural Beauty; 'The Runaway Reptiles' by Margaret Mahy from *Bubble Trouble and Other Poems and Stories*, published by Hamish Hamilton Ltd 1991, copyright © Margaret Mahy, 1991, reprinted by permission of Vanessa Hamilton Books Ltd; 'The Sword in the Stone' by T. H. White from *The Once and Future King*, published by Collins 1938, copyright © Lloyds Bank Trust Company (Channel Islands) Ltd, 1938, reprinted by permission of David Higham Associates.

Every effort has been made to trace copyright holders but in a few cases this has proved impossible. The editor and publishers apologize for these cases of copyright transgression and would like to hear from any copyright holder not acknowledged.

Wishing & Hoping.
forever & Ever.
Diana King

If you love someone
say it aloud
if not the moment will pass
you